IRON VALLEY

A Football Story About Belief, Brotherhood, and Second Chances

Kenny Simpson

This is a work of fiction. Any resemblance to actual persons or events is coincidental.

ISBN: 979-8-9953411-0-9

Printed in the United States of America

FOREWORD

Foreword by Chris Stevens, 32+ year football coaching veteran and co-founder of "The Friday Night Life" podcast

Iron Valley by Kenny Simpson is a compelling work of fiction that uses football as the backdrop for a much deeper story about life, relationships, and the culture surrounding Friday nights in small-town America.

High school football occupies a unique place in American culture. It exists at the intersection of community, adolescence, and competition, where Friday nights become something larger than the game itself. The lights, the band, the packed bleachers, and the nervous energy in a locker room full of teenagers all combine to create something that is hard to explain to someone who has never experienced it. It is not simply a sport. It is a shared ritual that binds players, coaches, families, and entire towns together.

That is what makes stories like Iron Valley resonate so deeply.

For those who have lived inside the world of high school football, the details ring true immediately. The early morning film sessions. The quiet bus rides home after a tough loss. The speeches that somehow land at just the right moment. The bond between players who come from different backgrounds but are united by a common goal. These experiences form the backbone of the game, but more importantly, they shape the people involved in it.
Fiction has a powerful ability to capture that world in ways statistics and records never can. A scoreboard tells you who won. A story tells you what it means.

In Iron Valley, readers will recognize the culture that makes high school football special. It is the culture of accountability, where every player understands his role in something bigger than himself. It is the culture of belief, where a team can begin the season uncertain and slowly grow into something stronger together. And it is the culture of resilience, where setbacks become lessons and adversity becomes fuel.

Players recognize themselves in these stories because they have lived them. Every player remembers the moment when football stopped being just a game and became something more, when they learned what it meant to push through fatigue, to trust a teammate, or to respond when things didn't go their way. Those lessons stay long after the final whistle of their last game.

Coaches (and spouses), perhaps even more so, understand the deeper layers of these stories. Coaching is rarely just about drawing plays on a whiteboard. It is about building belief in young people who are still discovering who they are. It is about creating an environment where effort matters, character matters, and the standards of the team become the standards of the individuals within it. And what it means to have a life balance within their own families while they co-raise other people's children for the better part of their formative years.

The best programs understand that culture always precedes results. Wins and losses may fluctuate, but a strong culture creates consistency. It teaches players how to prepare, how to respond to pressure, and how to carry themselves when the spotlight fades. Those lessons become part of who they are long after they leave the locker room.

That is why football matters beyond the field.

The game has a way of compressing life lessons into a few short months every year. It teaches discipline in the grind of daily practice. It teaches humility in defeat and gratitude in victory. It teaches young people that progress rarely happens overnight and that meaningful achievements require trust, sacrifice, and perseverance.

Many former players will tell you that years later they remember very few specific plays. What they remember instead are the people and the moments: the teammate who picked them up after a mistake, the coach who believed in them when they doubted themselves, the feeling of walking out under the lights knowing they were part of something meaningful.

Those memories are powerful because they represent growth.

Stories like Iron Valley remind us why the game continues to matter. They capture the emotion, the struggle, and the belief that defines the high school football experience. They remind us that while the games themselves may last only a few hours, the lessons can last a lifetime.

For readers who have stood on the sidelines, worn the uniform, coached the players, or cheered from the stands, this story will feel familiar. And for those encountering this world for the first time, it offers a glimpse into why so many people hold these Friday nights so close to their hearts.
Because at its best, high school football is never just about football.

It is about people. It is about growth. And most of all, it is about belief: belief in a team, belief in a culture, and belief in what young people can become when they commit themselves to something bigger than they ever imagined.

QUOTES

"Iron Valley by Kenny Simpson is a compelling work of fiction that uses football as the backdrop for a much deeper story about life, relationships, and the culture surrounding Friday nights in small-town America. While the game itself plays an important role, the heart of the book lies in the human experiences that unfold around it—ambition, sacrifice, loyalty, and the pressure that comes with representing something bigger than yourself.

What makes Iron Valley particularly engaging is that it doesn't limit its perspective to the coaches and players on the field. Simpson captures the full ecosystem of the Friday night experience: the spouses who support the long coaching hours, the assistant coaches grinding behind the scenes, the athletes chasing their dreams, and the fans filling the bleachers every week. Each perspective adds depth and authenticity to the story, making the football setting feel real and relatable.

This is not just a book for coaches or die-hard football enthusiasts. Anyone who has lived through the "Friday Night Life" in any capacity—whether as a spouse, athlete, assistant coach, or simply a loyal fan—will find something familiar and meaningful in its pages. In the end, Iron Valley reminds readers that football may bring people together, but it's the themes and rhythms of life, relationships, and shared experiences that leave the lasting impact."
Chris Stevens – The Friday Night Life

Kenny Simpson does a magnificent job of encapsulating the pressures, downfalls, and victories of high school football. This book allows us to peer inside the locker room, and understand that football is more about relationships than X's and O's.
Barry Grooms – Hooten's Arkansas Football

ACKNOWLEDGEMENTS

This book didn't come from one season, one team, or one idea.

It came from years of conversations, locker rooms, long drives home, and lessons learned the hard way. It was shaped by people who showed up when winning wasn't guaranteed, and by ideas that stayed useful long after the scoreboard stopped cooperating.

Several of the concepts, themes, and moments in this story were directly influenced by work I've written before. Not because those books provided answers, but because they helped frame better questions.

Coaching Football Like a Basketball Coach influenced how the game is taught throughout this story: teaching in layers, simplifying under pressure, and trusting structure to create freedom. Jack's approach to practice, in-game adjustment, and staff alignment grew out of those ideas.

Find a Way provided the backbone for the mindset that runs quietly through the book, the belief that progress comes from staying, adapting, and refusing to panic when circumstances aren't ideal.

Training for More Than the Game shaped the emphasis on weekly team themes, character development, and the understanding that football is often just the vehicle, not the destination.

0–10 To 10-0 informed the reality of failure shown here. Losing seasons, doubt, and the slow work of rebuilding are rarely glamorous, but they are often where the most important growth begins.

Beyond books, this story belongs to coaches who stayed when it would've been easier to leave.

To players who showed up carrying more than pads.
To assistants who taught quietly and corrected honestly.
To families who opened their homes, fed extra mouths, and made teams feel like something more than a roster.

It also belongs to my own family, especially my wife, my redeemer, who has lived every version of this work alongside me. Late nights. Through all the doubts. Through the wins that didn't fix everything. And the losses that taught more than victories ever could.

Iron Valley is fictional.
But the people who inspired it are not.

If you see yourself in these pages, that is the point of the book. I appreciate your support.

If you want the real story behind this book:

TABLE OF CONTENTS

CHAPTER ONE

The Scoreboard Doesn't Care

Present

The scoreboard flickered once before settling into its familiar glow.

IRON VALLEY — 0
HILLDALE — 42

Coach Jack Mercer stood near the sideline with his headset pushed halfway off one ear, the plastic biting into his neck. He didn't bother adjusting it anymore. There was nothing left to hear.

The fourth-quarter clock bled time in slow, deliberate seconds, each tick feeling personal. Across the field, Hilldale's starters laughed near the bench, helmets off, jerseys already loosening. Their backups jogged in eager and fresh, like this game was a reward instead of a burial. Iron Valley's sideline looked nothing like that. Helmets stayed on, heads down, pads sagging like they weighed more than they had an hour earlier.

Jack shoved his hands deeper into his jacket pockets, not because it was cold but because he didn't know what else to do with them. Clapping felt fake. Yelling felt pointless. Standing still felt like surrender.

He scanned the stands. They were already emptying. Parents clustered near the rail, arms crossed, murmuring into the night air. A few students lingered more out of habit than hope. The band played, but half the horns weren't raised. Even the fight song sounded tired.

Iron Valley football was supposed to mean something. Now it meant nights like this.

Jack's eyes found Tyler Briggs.

Senior guard. Three-year starter. Tyler sat on the bench with his helmet on the ground between his feet, elbows on his knees, staring straight ahead like he was trying to will the field into changing. Jack didn't need to ask about Tyler's history: three losing seasons, two coaching staffs, different coordinators, different systems. Same school.

Tyler never complained. Never pointed fingers. He just stayed.

Farther down the bench, linemen leaned against each other, chests heaving. A receiver stared at the field like it had personally betrayed him. Another kid kicked at the grass, like he might dig his way out.

Jack swallowed, his throat tightening in a slow, involuntary motion, his mouth tasting like copper and the flat remnants of old Gatorade. Overhead, the lights buzzed steadily, a sound he hadn't registered until now, when the silence underneath it felt louder than any crowd.

His jaw tightened until it ached. He realized he'd been holding his breath for the entire drive.

The whistle blew. Another snap. Another missed tackle. Hilldale's running back slipped through a gap that hadn't existed all week in practice, bounced outside, and jogged the last ten yards before flipping the ball to the official like it was a walkthrough rep.

42–0.

Jack closed his eyes longer than he should have. He'd imagined his first game this season plenty of times. The nerves, momentum swings, and losses that taught the team something. He hadn't pictured this.

"Coach."

Jack opened his eyes. Ray Holloway stood beside him, arms crossed, jaw tight.

"Starters are asking if they're done," Ray said.

Jack watched the defense jog back out, shoulders bracing for another hit.

"One more series," Jack said.

Ray hesitated. "You sure?"

"We don't quit."

Ray exhaled through his nose. "Just checking."

As Ray walked away, Jack felt the weight of the decision settle. He knew how it would look. Keeping starters in a blowout always did. But Jack wasn't thinking about optics.

Hilldale snapped the ball again. Another completion. Another missed assignment. Jack turned toward the far end of the bench and noticed Neil standing there, helmet buckled, chin strap tight, eyes locked on the field like every snap belonged to him. He leaned forward between plays, reacting before the whistle, studying everything like he planned to remember it later.

Jack filed it away.

The clock hit zero. The horn sounded: long, flat, final. Hilldale cheered. Iron Valley didn't move.

Jack stayed near midfield while the other coach crossed over. The handshake was quick and polite. Good luck the rest of the way.

Jack nodded, meaning none of it.

As the team headed toward the tunnel, Jack let them go ahead and lingered near the field, staring once more at the scoreboard. It didn't care about the summer, didn't care about last year's 0–10, didn't care that this was supposed to be different. It only told the truth.

Jack turned toward the tunnel.

That's when he heard voices, not players, but administrators.

"…can't go through another season like last year."

"He said it would take time."

A pause.

"If this turns into another 0–10…"

The voices faded as Jack passed. He wondered if he'd mistaken stubbornness for belief, and the thought followed him down the tunnel like an echo he couldn't shake.

Halfway down, footsteps fell in beside him.

"Coach."

Jack knew the voice.

"I'm sorry," Cole said quietly. "Everything felt fast. Like I was late to everything."

Jack studied him. Frustration. Embarrassment. Fear. But not quitting.

"That's because you're trying to survive plays instead of understanding them. The game is moving too fast for you right now," Jack said.

Cole nodded, even though Jack knew the lesson wouldn't settle tonight. Jack rested a hand briefly on his shoulder, not a pat, something steadier.

"We'll fix it," Jack said. "But not tonight."

Cole exhaled. "Okay, Dad. I just don't want to be the reason…" He trailed off.

Inside the locker room, the air was thick with sweat, rubber, and silence. Helmets hit the floor harder than necessary. Pads thudded. Nobody spoke.

Jack waited until the noise faded, then set his headset on the bench.

"I'm not going to yell," he said. "You've been yelled at enough. We got it handed to us tonight. It ain't about heart. You showed up. It's about identity. We're still figuring out who we are on that field. And yeah… that starts with me."

A few heads lifted.

"If you're looking for a coach who'll promise wins, I'm not your guy," Jack continued. "And if you're looking for someone who'll quit when it gets hard, I'm not your guy either."

Ray leaned against the wall, arms folded. He didn't nod. He didn't argue.

"Go home," Jack said. "Monday, we get back after it."

Players drifted out in small groups, shoulder pads creaking and cleats scraping softly on the concrete. No one talked much, and when a helmet slipped from someone's hand and hit the floor, the hollow sound seemed louder than it should have been. The stadium lights hummed overhead, and the place felt abandoned, like even the night had moved on.

Jack stepped back onto the field once the locker room emptied. The scoreboard still glowed.

42–0.

One of the seniors stood near the sideline, helmet in his hands, staring at the empty field like he wasn't ready to leave it yet. Jack recognized the look. It wasn't anger or disappointment anymore.

It was fatigue.

This wasn't just a loss. It was another in a line that had grown too long to ignore: twenty-seven in a row now.

Jack exhaled slowly, hands on his hips, eyes still on the field. Losing once hurts, but losing for years settles into a place deeper than frustration until it becomes expectation, and expectation is the hardest thing to beat.

He realized something then that he hadn't admitted to himself before. It wasn't the scoreboard that beat you after a while. It was the silence afterward.

The lights began shutting off row by row, darkness moving across the field like a curtain closing. The scoreboard was black now, the lights dimmed, and the silence stayed.

Jack turned toward the tunnel.

"It's not the bottom," he said quietly.
"It just feels like it."

And for the first time that night, he believed it.

CHAPTER TWO

When Hope Shows Up Early

Two Years Ago

Hope arrived before Jack Mercer ever coached a practice. It came with the job.

Before a single kid ran a route or lifted a weight. It came with handshakes, newspaper blurbs, and a quiet buzz that followed him everywhere he went.

This guy's different.
Did you see what he did at Pine Ridge?
Finally, someone who knows how to win.

Jack heard it in the grocery store. At the gas station. In the stands during summer workouts. People said his name like it already meant something to them.

It did. Just not here yet.

Jack hadn't gone looking for Iron Valley. The job had found him midseason, while Pine Ridge was winning. Playoffs locked. Confidence everywhere. The kind of stability coaches weren't supposed to leave.

But Iron Valley kept calling.

And then it went wrong at Pine Ridge. Wins matter, but politics matter more, and Jack found out the hard way that he was not very good at politics. When he was told to play certain players or start looking for a new job, the choice wasn't very difficult.

So, he picked up the phone and called Iron Valley back as soon as the season was over.

The interview room had tried too hard. Fresh paint over old walls. Framed photos from decades ago: leather helmets, state trophies that felt like artifacts instead of history.

"We have tradition," the superintendent had said.

Jack nodded politely.

Tradition without belief was just memory.

The superintendent leaned forward, fingers laced on the table.

"We've had four head coaches in six years," he said. "What makes you think you'll last longer than they did?"

The room went quiet.

Jack didn't answer right away. He'd learned a long time ago that quick answers to hard questions usually sounded rehearsed.

"I don't chase quick fixes," he said finally. "I build habits that outlast me. But that takes time…and it takes everybody in this room deciding we're going to stay steady when things don't turn fast."

The superintendent studied him, then leaned back.

The athletic director spoke next.

"Our kids deal with a lot," he said. "Some of them go home to things that matter more than football. How do you coach when life hits harder than practice?"

Jack thought about that one longer, about the players he'd coached before. About long bus rides. About the quiet conversations that happened after games when everyone else had gone home.

"Football's just the vehicle to help influence kids," he said. "The real work is showing up when the game's over. If kids know you're there for that, they'll give you everything they've got between the lines."

No one spoke for a moment.

Then the superintendent nodded once, like he'd heard what he needed to hear.

The athletic director closed the folder in front of him, then leaned back slightly.

"We would like to keep some of the staff," he said. "There are a few guys who've been here a while. Good relationships with the kids. One in particular, Holloway. He's our defensive coordinator. He has been loyal to our school and is from the area."

Jack nodded, listening.

"He interviewed for the head job," the AD added. "We felt, after a winless season, it was hard to hand the program to someone already inside it. Fair or not, that's just how those decisions go."

The superintendent folded his hands on the table. "We do think it would be good for the program if he stayed. There's value in continuity, especially for the players."

Jack nodded again. "I'd want to meet him."

"You will," the athletic director said.

The conversation moved on, but the name stayed with Jack.

A defensive coordinator who had interviewed for the job. From a staff that had just gone winless.

Continuity sounded good in a conference room.

On a sideline, it could mean something different.

Jack made a quiet note to himself.

He'd need to see it up close.

They talked culture. Accountability. Jack had rebuilt before. He knew what it took.

What he noticed were the looks.

The pauses after his answers.
The unspoken *Are you sure you want this?*

Near the end, the athletic director leaned back.

"We've struggled," he said carefully. "For a long time."

Jack nodded.

"And five miles up the road…" The AD didn't finish.

He didn't need to.

West Ridge.

Same county. Same kids. Same resources. Different results.

West Ridge won.
Iron Valley endured.

"We don't expect miracles, we just want to compete with those guys," the superintendent added.

Jack almost laughed.

The drive home was quiet. Megan watched the road roll past the windshield. Cole and Bennett, the youngest, sat in the back seat, earbuds in, unaware their lives were about to change.

Jack slowed the truck as he passed the old mill. Its smokestacks stood like headstones against the November sky, cold and silent. He looked toward the corner store where a 'Go Wolves' banner hung limp; it was so frayed and bleached by the sun it looked more like a white flag of surrender than a rallying cry.

He realized then that in Iron Valley, winning wasn't just about a scoreboard; it was the only thing that kept the ghosts of the 1980 state championship from mocking the men standing in the unemployment line.

"You'd take it," Megan said finally.

Jack exhaled. "It's a mess."

"So was Pine Ridge."

"That was different."

"How?"

Jack thought about the film he'd watched. The late-game body language. The way Iron Valley kids seemed to brace for failure before it arrived.

"They don't believe," he said. "Not really."

Megan nodded. "Neither did Pine Ridge."

At Pine Ridge, kids argued over reps. At Iron Valley, they waited to be told where to stand.

Cole's reflection flickered in the rearview mirror. Eighth grade. Strong. Fast. Football still simple.

Iron Valley would be his school now.

The offer came two days later.

Jack accepted it that night.

Moving across state lines felt heavier than expected. Boxes. Goodbyes. New faces. Megan handled it quietly. Cole didn't complain. Bennett was excited to be part of the whole process.

After doing his research about the area, Cole quickly found out that West Ridge was the school of choice for great athletes.

"Am I playing for you?" Cole asked once.

Jack nodded. "You're playing for Iron Valley."

Cole nodded. That was enough.

• • •

Jack stepped out of the field house and walked toward the stadium alone.

The place was quiet. No music. No whistles. Just the sound of wind pushing through the trees beyond the far end zone.

The bleachers showed their age. Paint faded. A few boards warped. The press box windows looked like they hadn't been cleaned in years.

Near the entrance hung a banner from the only state championship.

Nineteen eighty.

Jack stood there a moment longer than he meant to.

Tradition was still here, but belief wasn't.

He walked down to the field and stood at the numbers, looking across the empty turf. It wasn't a bad field. It wasn't a great one either. It just felt… tired.

Somewhere in the distance, a car door slammed. A dog barked. Then it was quiet again.

Jack put his hands on his hips and looked around one more time.

This place didn't need speeches. It needed time, and someone willing to endure what it would take to get it back on track.

• • •

One year ago

The first summer felt electric.

Workouts were full. The weight room stayed loud long after the last set. Players lingered on the field, throwing routes while the sun slipped behind the bleachers.

Parents leaned against the fence and stayed late, talking about the season like it was already on its way.

Kids talked about winning before pads ever came on.

Jack didn't stop it.
Didn't correct it.

He believed work would catch up.

The lifts. The reps. The film sessions. The hours stacked on top of each other like bricks.

He thought great effort would be enough to carry them when the lights came on.

He didn't consider that there was more to belief than just working hard.

He would soon learn.

CHAPTER THREE

Work Isn't Enough

Last Season

Fridays always felt different.

The field house smelled like barbecue and sweat, the way it always did before games. Folding tables lined the wall. Helmets sat under chairs. Music played just loud enough to keep the nerves from creeping in too early.

Jack stood near the door, clipboard in hand, doing what he always did, counting heads without making it obvious. Evan was missing.

Jack checked his watch. They were ten minutes into the team meal.

Enough time for it to be noticed.

Evan wasn't a problem kid. Sophomore. Backup receiver. Quiet. Didn't draw attention to himself. But he'd been late a few times over the past couple of weeks: two, maybe three. Nothing dramatic. Enough that Jack had already handled it.

Extra runs. Extra gassers. No complaints.

Jack believed in progressive discipline. Kids deserved chances, as long as the standard stayed clear.

He scanned the room again.

Still no Evan.

An assistant leaned toward him. "You want me to text him?"

Jack shook his head. "No."

Friday wasn't about chasing kids down. Friday was about expectation.

The room buzzed. Parents served plates. Players joked and laughed, trying to act loose while pretending they weren't watching the door too.

Jack felt the moment tightening.

Then Evan slipped in, late again, breathing hard, hoodie half-zipped, eyes already apologizing.

"Coach—" Evan started.

Jack raised a hand.

Evan stopped. Not arguing. Just… stopped. His chest still rising and falling, something frantic sitting just behind his eyes.

For a second, Jack held there.

There was something in the kid's face. Not defiance. Not carelessness.

Something else.

Jack felt it.

And ignored it.

Evan shifted his weight. "Coach, I—"

"Bring me your helmet," he said. Calm. Even.

The room went quiet faster than it had all season.

Evan froze. "Coach, I—"

"You've already been run this week," Jack said. "We're past that."

Evan swallowed. "I just—"

"Not tonight," Jack said.

No yelling. No explanation. No debate.

The message was clean.

Friday matters.
Being on time matters.
Culture matters more than convenience.

Evan walked to the far wall and sat, plate untouched.

A few players watched. A few parents noticed. An assistant nodded once.

That's leadership, Jack told himself.

The meal finished. Helmets went on. The locker room snapped back into rhythm.

Iron Valley played harder that night than they had in weeks.

They still lost.

But nobody questioned effort.

After the game, Ray stopped Jack near the tunnel.

"Good call tonight," he said. "Kids need to know standards aren't optional."

Jack nodded.

He believed it.

• • •

Monday morning, Evan wasn't at school.

Jack stood in front of the locker.

Helmet gone.
Cleats gone.
Nameplate peeled off.

He exhaled slowly.

Kids quit sometimes. It happened.

But something about the empty space bothered him in a way he couldn't explain.

He closed the locker door and walked into the office.

"Anybody heard from Evan?" he asked.

A couple of assistants shook their heads.

"Probably embarrassed," Ray said. "Some kids don't come back after sitting out."

Jack nodded.

That made sense.

It just didn't feel right.

That night, Jack sat at the kitchen table longer than usual.

He kept seeing the Friday meal.

Evan standing in the doorway.
Trying to speak.
Jack raising a hand to stop him.

He told himself it was the right call.

Standards mattered.

Still… something in the kid's face had looked less like guilt and more like worry.

Jack pushed the thought away.

But it came back anyway.

• • •

Later in the week, as they were getting ready for another game, near the end of the meeting, Jack asked it casually.

"Anyone hear from Evan?"

Chairs shifted.

One assistant leaned back. "He and Tyler were pretty close. Haven't seen him around."

Another coach hesitated before speaking.

"I heard his mom's schedule changed again," he said. "Kid's basically raising his little brother most nights."

The room went quiet.

No one looked at Jack.

Jack nodded once and moved the meeting on.

But he didn't hear much of the rest of it.

• • •

That Thursday, Jack got paged to see the counselor.

The counselor closed the door gently.

"Evan wasn't late because he forgot," she said.

Jack didn't speak.

"He walks his brother to school every morning. Mom works nights. Sometimes she doesn't make it home."

Jack stared at the floor.

"I wish I'd known that," Jack muttered.

She looked him directly in the eyes.

"He thought explaining wouldn't matter," she said. "He didn't think you'd change your mind."

Jack nodded once.

Not because he agreed.

Because he didn't trust himself to speak.

The standard he believed in suddenly felt less like structure and more like a wall.

After the counselor closed the door, Jack stared at the floor until the tile pattern blurred.

He thought about driving by Evan's house: not to knock, not to explain. Just to see a light on. Just to know the kid was alright.

He didn't.

But the thought followed him the rest of the day, quiet and steady, like a sound you only notice when everything else goes silent.

• • •

A few weeks later, Jack found Tyler taping his wrists before practice.

"You still talk to Evan?" Jack asked.

Tyler nodded. "Sometimes."

"How's he doing?"

Tyler shrugged. "Working some. Taking care of his brother."

Jack nodded.

"If you see him," Jack said, "tell him I'd like to talk. No pressure. Just… tell him."

Tyler studied him for a second, then nodded again.

"Yes, sir."

Jack watched him jog back to the line, feeling the weight settle again: not sharp like guilt, but steady like something unfinished.

• • •

The season ended without a win.

0–10.

No asterisks. No moral victories that survived the drive home.

Just ten Fridays where Iron Valley fought and came up short.

Some losses were close. Too close. One-score games that slipped late. A missed tackle. A blown assignment. A bounce that never went their way.

There were nights when they almost broke through.

The October rain at Riverside, where they led for forty-six minutes, only to watch a fourteen-point lead disappear in three plays because someone made a small mistake, which led to a last-second loss.

But Homecoming was the one that stayed.

Week six. Iron Valley had lost five straight to start the season, each one bleeding into the next until the losses stopped feeling separate and started feeling like a condition. But Homecoming carried a different energy. The hallways buzzed all week. Students painted banners. Teachers wore school colors without being asked. The band practiced extra. Parents volunteered for the cookout. Even the weather cooperated, cool, clear, the kind of Friday that reminded people why they used to love this.

Jack felt it too, and he didn't trust it.

He had spent the week game-planning harder than he had all season. He knew the opponent inside and out, their tendencies, their weaknesses, where their secondary cheated, how their linebackers fit the run. He had the right scheme. He believed that completely. For the first time all year, the film work and the practice reps lined up perfectly. The kids had it. He could see it in walkthroughs. Clean reads. Decisive feet. No hesitation.

By Thursday, Jack caught himself thinking something dangerous.

We're going to win this one.

He pushed the thought away. Then it came back. He pushed it away again.

Friday arrived and the stands filled earlier than they had all season. The parking lot ran out of spaces. People stood along the fence three deep. The press box, usually half-empty, had every seat taken. For one night, Iron Valley looked like a program that believed in itself.

Jack walked the sideline during warmups and noticed something he hadn't seen all year. The kids were loose. Not careless, but loose the way teams get when the preparation removes the doubt. Tyler called out blocking assignments before coaches could. Receivers ran crisp routes without being told to reset. Even the younger players moved with purpose.

The game started and Iron Valley played the best football they had played all season.

The defense held on the opening drive. The offense moved the ball with patience, inside zone, a quick hitch, play-action for a chunk play that moved the chains past midfield. Jack's gameplan was working. Every tendency he had identified on film showed up exactly the way he expected. The opposing defensive coordinator kept adjusting, and every adjustment played into something Jack had already prepared for.

I'm outcoaching him, Jack thought midway through the second quarter. He didn't say it. Didn't need to. It was just there, sitting quietly behind every play call like a fact he was afraid to acknowledge.

Iron Valley scored first. A clean drive. Twelve plays. No penalties. The sideline erupted.

Then they scored again.

By halftime, Iron Valley led 14–3, and something strange had settled over the stadium. Hope. Not the cautious kind that showed up before the season. The real kind. The kind that made people stand a little taller and talk a little louder and forget, just for a few minutes, how many Fridays had ended the other way.

Jack stood in the locker room at halftime and looked at his team. They weren't nervous. They weren't tight. They were playing the way he had always believed they could.

And somewhere in the back of his mind, a voice he couldn't silence whispered: *So how do we lose this one?*

The third quarter was a grind. The opponent adjusted. Slowed the tempo. Shortened the field. Jack expected it. He had told the staff at halftime they would tighten up, they would try to make it ugly, don't panic, just keep executing.

They kept executing.

Midway through the third quarter, the opponent put together a decent drive and punched it in from the six. 14–10. The crowd shifted, but Iron Valley's sideline didn't flinch. They had expected a response. This was still their game.

Then it happened.

Second and eight from the opponent's own thirty. A short crossing route, nothing special, the kind of play that gains six yards and everyone forgets about it. The safety read it perfectly. He jumped the route, got both hands on the ball, and it bounced straight up off his palms, hung in the air for what felt like forever, and came down in the arms of a receiver who had no business being open. He caught it in stride at the forty with nothing but green grass in front of him.

Seventy yards. Untouched.

The visiting bleachers erupted. The Iron Valley sideline stood frozen, watching the replay on the scoreboard like the film might show a different ending.

17–14.

Jack stared at the field and felt something shift underneath him, not in the game, but in the air. In the body language on the bench. In the way helmets tilted just slightly lower and shoulders curled inward like the cold had suddenly gotten worse.

He had seen this before. Not the play itself, but the feeling afterward. The slow creep of history reminding everyone in the stadium what always happened next.

Not this time, he told himself.

Iron Valley's defense stiffened the rest of the third quarter. The offense settled. Tyler was playing the best game of his career, finishing blocks that turned two-yard runs into five-yard runs, resetting the line of scrimmage play after play.

Then the drive came.

Late fourth quarter. Iron Valley took over near their own thirty with a chance to take the lead back. Jack called it the way he'd drawn it up all week. Inside run. Counter. Quick pass to move the sticks. The ball moved steadily downfield while the clock bled.

First down inside the ten.

The crowd stood.

Second down at the four. A run that gained three yards. Bodies piling up. The whistle blew.

First and goal from the one.

The stadium noise changed. Not louder, but fuller. The kind of sound that comes from people who hadn't had anything to cheer for in years finally believing they were about to see it happen.

Jack sent in the play. Power right. Tyler's side. Simple. Decisive. The same play they had run a hundred times in practice.

The center set his feet. The quarterback crouched under center.

Jack held his breath.

The snap came low.

Not wildly low. Just enough. The quarterback reached for it and the ball skipped off his fingertips and bounced sideways on the turf. For half a second, nobody moved. Then everyone moved at once, and the wrong jersey came up with it.

Fumble.

The sound that followed wasn't a groan or a gasp. It was silence. The kind that presses in from every direction at once and makes the stadium feel twice as large and completely empty at the same time.

Jack watched the referee signal the recovery and felt something disconnect behind his ribs.

The opponent ran out the clock from there. Three runs and a punt. It didn't matter. The game was already over, and everyone in the stadium knew it before the horn confirmed it. Final score, 17–14.

The handshake line moved slowly. The other coach said something Jack didn't hear. The walk to the locker room felt longer than it should have.

Jack didn't speak to the team. He tried once, opened his mouth, and nothing came out that felt worth saying. He just stood there while the silence did its work, and then he told them to get cleaned up.

Tyler sat on the bench for twenty minutes after everyone else had left. Jack saw him through the office window and didn't go out. Some moments weren't his to interrupt.

• • •

The drive home was quiet.

Megan sat in the passenger seat watching the road. She hadn't said anything since they left the stadium. Bennett was already asleep in the back. Cole sat with his earbuds in, staring out the window, replaying something behind his eyes.

Jack's hands gripped the wheel tighter than necessary.

"I knew it," he said finally.

Megan looked over.

"I knew we'd find a way. Somewhere in the back of my head the whole game, I knew it." His voice was flat, not angry, just tired in a way that went deeper than one Friday night. "I had the perfect gameplan. I'm outcoaching that guy tonight, Megan. Our kids played harder than they've played all year. And it doesn't matter."

She didn't respond right away.

"We had first and goal from the one-yard line," he continued, "and we couldn't execute a snap. A snap. The most basic thing in football."

He exhaled hard.

"I can scheme it right. I can teach it right. I can put them in every position to win. And they still can't finish it, because something in this program doesn't believe it's allowed to."

The words hung in the truck cab.

Megan was quiet for a long time.

"That's not something a gameplan fixes," she said.

Jack stared at the road.

"I know," he said. "That's what scares me."

They drove the rest of the way in silence.

That loss stayed with him the longest. Not because of the score. Because for three quarters he had seen exactly who they could become, and then watched them remember who they still were.

The 0–10 wasn't just a lack of points.

It was a slow-motion wreck where everyone could see the wall coming, and no one believed they could turn the wheel.

One night after a loss, the locker room stayed quiet longer than usual.

Not angry quiet.
Not defeated quiet.
Just tired.

Helmets rested on the floor. Shoulder pads leaned against lockers. No one rushed to shower. No one joked.

Tyler sat on the bench, elbows on his knees, staring at the floor like he was replaying every snap in his head.

Across the room, a sophomore kicked his tape roll across the tile and immediately looked ashamed of himself.

Jack didn't give a speech.

He just stood there a moment and finally said, "Get cleaned up. We'll be back Monday."

A few players nodded.

Most didn't look up.

On the bus ride home, no one played music.

Half the team stared out the windows. Some slept sitting upright, heads against cold glass, the red glow of brake lights washing across their faces every few seconds. A couple of players laughed at something on a phone, the sound out of place in the dark bus.

Jack sat near the front and realized something he hadn't expected.

They weren't angry anymore. They were starting to expect it. And that was worse.

Some of the losses were ugly.

Jack owned all of them.

He stood in front of the team after the final game and didn't sugarcoat it.

"This one's on me," he said.

They nodded.

They always did.

The final game ended the way too many others had that season. Fourth quarter. One score. A missed tackle that turned into forty yards and a touchdown. Just like that, the night and the season were over.

• • •

The winter that followed felt different from what Jack expected. Not louder. Quieter. Heavier.

Tyler came up to Jack that offseason and said,
"Evan said to tell you he's good."

Jack nodded.

Then Tyler added:
"He said he never quit on the team. Just couldn't make both worlds work."

That stung. Going 0–10 was awful, but making a kid have to pick between family and football was worse.

Staff meetings dragged. Conversations circled the same places: schemes, tweaks, offseason plans. Everyone worked. No one felt aligned.

Jack realized something uncomfortable.

They had been busy.
They had not been connected.

He hadn't introduced team themes that first year. Hadn't slowed down to teach meaning. He told himself they needed football first.

In truth, he didn't yet know how to lead them through losing.

• • •

Cole didn't carry the same weight.

He played junior high ball that season. That team was decent. Competitive. They won games. Cole played well, naturally, easily.

Jack was responsible for that staff, too. The junior high coaches reported to him. Practice plans passed across his desk. Depth charts, schedules, and equipment requests all fed through the same system.

The junior high program fed the high school. It always had.

And now it was his to oversee.

Still, most nights Jack kept his distance.

After varsity practice, he would walk over and stand near the fence while the junior high finished up under the lights. Close enough to watch. Far enough not to interfere.

He told himself he didn't want to step on the coaches' toes.

The truth was, it was easier to watch from the outside.

Cole moved differently from most kids his age. Calm in the huddle. Quick with the ball. Confident without needing to show it. When something broke down, he didn't panic. He just found space and kept moving.

The other parents cheered loudly. Kids slapped helmets and jogged back to the sideline, smiling.

It looked easy.

Jack leaned against the fence and felt pride settle in first. Then something else followed it. Guilt.

His son was learning how to win, but his program didn't know how yet.

One night after a game, the junior high head coach walked past him on the way to the field house.

"Good group," the coach said. "They compete."

Jack nodded. "They do."

"They'll help you in a couple of years."

Jack watched the kids laughing near the buses.

"I hope so," he said quietly.

He stayed at the fence a little longer after the field lights went out.

It wasn't the winning that stayed with him.

It felt so natural to those kids.

No tension. No history pressing down on them. No weight of last year or the year before that.

Just football.

Jack turned and walked back toward the varsity field, where the grass was worn thinner and the lights always seemed a little harsher.

• • •

Then, the move to 4A came that winter.

Bigger schools. Bigger rosters. Less margin.

After going 0–20 in 3A the past two seasons, Iron Valley would return to 4A.

Jack sat at the kitchen table, schedule spread out, Cole doing homework nearby. Megan watched him longer than usual.

"Still glad we came?" she asked.

Jack stared at the paper.

"Yes," he said finally. "But I know why it went wrong now."

Megan waited.

"We worked hard," Jack said. "But we don't stand for anything yet."

She nodded.

Jack flipped back through his old practice plans.

Conditioning blocks.
Periods timed to the minute.
Rep counts.

Everything was measured. Then he noticed what wasn't written anywhere.

Nothing about why they were doing any of it.

Jack closed the notebook and sat there for a long time.

Later that night, Jack opened a notebook he hadn't touched all season and stared at the empty pages.

He didn't draw plays. He wrote words.

Simple ones and hard ones.

Words that meant more than football.

He didn't know it yet, but that notebook would become the backbone of everything Iron Valley would become.

Because work alone hadn't saved them.

And next time, it wouldn't be all they brought.

CHAPTER FOUR

You Don't Get to Choose the Weight

Preseason

Jack noticed it before Cole did.

That was usually how it went.

Cole Mercer walked onto the Iron Valley campus like he belonged there. Head up. Backpack slung over one shoulder. Too calm for a freshman. Too confident for a new kid. He didn't talk much, but he didn't hide either.

The other kids noticed him immediately. Not because he was the coach's son, but because he moved differently.

In PE. In the hallway. On the field behind the school after class. There was an ease to the way he ran, the way he cut, the way he caught a ball without breaking stride. Coaches noticed that kind of thing. So did players.

Talent travels fast.

The junior group went 6–3 last season. Most of the touchdowns came through Cole.

Jack saw it with clearer eyes now, eyes sharpened by an 0–10 season that had stripped away illusions. Losing had a way of making you honest about what mattered and what didn't.

By the end of the first week of offseason workouts, Cole had been tested.

Not with words, but with reps.

Extra pushes. Late contact. A little too much at the end of drills. The kind of quiet pressure older kids applied when they were deciding whether someone belonged.

Cole didn't complain, just kept showing up.

Jack watched it from a distance. He forced himself to. Being the head coach meant seeing everything and reacting to almost nothing. Being a father meant fighting every instinct to step in.

As a freshman, Cole earned his place the only way kids ever really do.

He beat them.

Not loud. Not flashy. Just consistently.

One-on-ones. Sprints. Conditioning. When it mattered, Cole showed up. When it didn't, he didn't disappear.

By the third week, the whispers had changed.

Coach's kid can play.
He's different.

Acceptance followed. Not friendship yet. But respect.

That night, Jack found Cole in the garage, throwing a football against the wall, catching it clean, over and over.

"You good?" Jack asked.

Cole shrugged. "Yeah."

Jack leaned against the doorframe. "You don't have to carry anything extra because of me."

Cole stopped throwing and looked at him. "I know."

Jack nodded.

They both wanted to believe that.

Practice ended late the next afternoon. Heat clung to the field. Kids dragged themselves toward the locker room. Jack stayed out, talking with assistants, already thinking about changes for next year, when he noticed a kid lingering near the fence.

Marcus Reed.

Sophomore. Receiver. Quiet. Talented in bursts. Inconsistent everywhere else.

Jack knew that look now. The look of a kid who wasn't ready to go home.

"Marcus," Jack called. "You good?"

Marcus nodded too fast. "Yes, sir."

Jack waited.

Silence had a way of doing the work for him.

Marcus finally looked down. "Can I stay a little?"

Jack nodded. "Grab a ball."

They threw routes in the fading light. Nothing fancy. Slants. Outs. Footwork. Jack didn't correct much.

He listened.

Eventually, Marcus stopped catching the ball and just stood there.

"My mom's not coming home tonight," he said.

Jack didn't ask why.

He just told him to come over for dinner.

Megan didn't ask questions when Jack walked in with Marcus.

She never did.

She handed the kid a plate of food as if she had been expecting him.

Cole glanced up from the table. Took it in. Said nothing.

They ate quietly. Marcus relaxed inch by inch, like his body finally believed it was allowed to stop bracing.

After dinner, Marcus sat on the couch while Cole tossed him a controller.

"You play?" Cole asked.

Marcus nodded. "Yeah."

They played for hours.

Jack drove Marcus home, if you could call it that. It was a small house that needed a lot more TLC to even be considered decent.

When Marcus got out, he hesitated.

"Coach?" he said.

Jack looked at him.

"Thank you."

Jack nodded. "See you tomorrow."

Driving home, Jack felt the familiar pull in his chest—the reminder that football was never the hard part.

For the first time, Jack wondered which role would cost him more, being a good coach or being a good father.

Coaching had always been clean to him. Standards. Consequences. Lines you didn't cross.

Fatherhood wasn't like that.

It didn't come with a playbook. No clear right answer. Just moments where doing nothing felt as heavy as doing something wrong.

Jack realized then that the discipline he trusted on the field might not protect his son from everything off it.

And that scared him more than losing ever had.

The field was easy, but life wasn't.

Megan was waiting when he walked in.

"He okay?" she asked.

Jack shook his head. "Not really."

She nodded. "He will be."

Later that night, Jack sat at the kitchen table, notebook open, untouched.

He thought about the weight his son carried—being good enough to be accepted and strong enough to be resented.

He thought about kids like Marcus, who showed up every day carrying more than pads and expectations.

He thought about the season that had just ended. About how hard they'd worked. About how little that alone had mattered.

He looked at the words he'd written earlier that week while planning the next year.

ACCOUNTABILITY
DISCIPLINE
EFFORT

All good words.

None of them was enough by itself.

Jack rubbed his eyes.

What if writing words on a whiteboard doesn't matter when a kid goes home to what Marcus goes home to?
What if you're just a football coach pretending this is bigger than it is?
What if effort and character are just things coaches say when the scoreboard doesn't cooperate?

He closed the notebook.

Tomorrow, they'd work fundamentals again: blocking angles, footwork, teaching coaches to slow down and teach instead of correcting.

But tonight reminded him of something else.

You don't get to choose the weight kids bring with them.

You only get to decide whether you help carry it.

And whether you're strong enough to keep walking.

CHAPTER FIVE
Marcus

The house was quiet when Marcus woke up.

Not the good kind of quiet. Not the kind that meant everyone was still asleep and the morning had not started yet. This quiet felt empty.

He lay still for a moment on the mattress on the floor, staring at the thin line of light slipping through the edge of the curtain. The room smelled like old carpet and laundry that had dried too long on a chair. Somewhere in the house, the refrigerator hummed and then clicked off again.

Marcus rolled onto his side and checked his phone.

6:12.

He sat up slowly so he would not wake his brother.

Dylan was asleep on the couch in the living room, one arm hanging off the side, the blanket twisted around his legs. The television was still on, silent blue light flickering across the walls. Marcus reached over and turned it off before walking into the kitchen.

The refrigerator opened with a tired creak.

Inside sat a nearly empty jar of jelly and a gallon of milk with maybe a glass left in it.

Nothing else.

Marcus closed the door and opened the cabinet. Bread and peanut butter waited on the shelf. He stood there a moment, staring at them like something else might appear behind the jar if he waited long enough.

It did not.

He laid two pieces of bread on the counter and spread peanut butter slowly across them, careful to reach the edges so the sandwich would feel like more than it was. When he finished, he wrapped them in paper towels and set them side by side.

One for him. One for Dylan.

He had been doing this every morning for a while now. Making lunch while the house was quiet and the hunger was still manageable. It was not something he thought about much anymore. Just something that had to be done.

Marcus wrote a D on one paper towel with a pen so they would not get mixed up.

Even though they always tasted the same.

Behind him, Dylan shifted on the couch.

"You up?" his brother mumbled.

"Yeah," Marcus said. "Get dressed. Bus comes in twenty."

Dylan rubbed his eyes and sat up. "Mom home?"

Marcus shook his head. "Not yet."

Dylan nodded and walked toward the bedroom without asking anything else.

That was the part Marcus hated most.

Not the empty kitchen. Not the quiet house. The way it all felt normal to his brother now.

• • •

The bus ride was loud the way buses always were. Kids talked across the aisles. Someone played music through a phone speaker. A couple of freshmen laughed too hard at something nobody else understood.

Marcus sat near the back and watched houses slide past the window.

He wondered sometimes what other mornings felt like. Hot breakfasts. Parents rushing kids out the door. Someone reminding you to grab your backpack before you forgot it.

He did not think about it long.

Thinking about things you did not have rarely helped. School passed the way school usually did. Marcus listened enough to keep up with the lessons, but his eyes drifted to the clock more than the board. Time moved differently on practice days.

It moved like something you had to get through before you could get somewhere that made sense.

• • •

Practice was the only place where things felt clear.

Routes were right or they were wrong. You caught the ball or you did not. You lined up correctly or the coaches told you where to stand.

The rules were simple. The expectations were simple.

Marcus liked that.

That afternoon he stayed after again, just like he had been doing most days. He ran routes by himself, catching balls from the machine and tossing them back into the net. The steady rhythm of footballs hitting the padding echoed across the field.

The sun dipped lower behind the bleachers, stretching long shadows across the turf.

Out here nobody asked questions he did not want to answer.

Out here he was just Marcus.

Not the kid making sandwiches every morning. Not the kid making sure his brother got to school. Not the kid pretending everything at home was fine.

Just Marcus.

And that felt like breathing.

• • •

The house was darker than usual when he got home that evening.

No lights. No television. No sound.

Dylan sat at the kitchen table doing homework, pressing his pencil so hard it nearly tore the paper.

"You eat?" Marcus asked.

Dylan shook his head.

Marcus opened the cabinet again and stared at the same two things waiting there.

Bread.
Peanut butter.

He made the sandwiches the same way he had that morning, spreading the peanut butter carefully and cutting one in half for Dylan. They ate quietly at the table, chewing slowly.

"Practice good?" Dylan asked.

"Yeah," Marcus said.

"You score?"

Marcus smiled a little. "Not today."

Dylan nodded like that made sense.

Afterward, Marcus washed the knife and wiped the counter even though it was not dirty. Little habits that made the kitchen feel more like a home than it actually was.

Later, Dylan fell asleep on the couch again.

Marcus covered him with a blanket and turned off the kitchen light, leaving the lamp in the corner glowing softly.

For a long time he sat at the table staring at nothing.

Sometimes the house felt so quiet it pressed against his ears.
Sometimes he stayed awake longer than he needed to just so he would not have to lie there listening to it.

• • •

The next afternoon, Marcus lingered at the field again after practice.

Most of the team had already gone inside, but he stayed on the bench with his helmet beside him, watching the empty field. The sun dropped slowly behind the bleachers, turning everything gold.

The air smelled like grass and sweat.

Quiet.
Not the empty kind.
The good kind.

Dylan's peewee practice was finishing soon, and Marcus planned to walk him home.

He heard footsteps on the gravel and glanced up. Coach Mercer was walking across the field toward the building.

Marcus looked back down quickly.

"You good?" Jack asked.

Marcus nodded too fast. "Yes sir."

Jack stood there a moment longer.

"Can I stay a little?" Marcus asked.

Jack gestured toward the ball rack. "Grab one."

They threw routes for a while. Nothing complicated. Just timing and footwork. Marcus ran the patterns and Jack tossed the ball right where it needed to be.

After a few minutes Marcus slowed down.
"My mom has not been home in a few days," he said.

Jack stayed quiet.

"She does that sometimes. Leaves for a while."

Jack had heard versions of this before. It never got easier.

"Where you heading after this?" Jack asked.

Marcus shrugged. "Store, I guess. Need to get food for me and Dylan."

Jack studied him for a moment.

"Come eat with us," he said. "Then we will get you something to take home."

Marcus hesitated.

Not because he did not want to go.

Because he was not used to people offering twice.

Jack waited.

Marcus nodded. "Okay."

• • •

Megan was already moving when Jack walked in with Marcus and Dylan.

She never needed to be told.
She set plates on the table like it was the most normal thing in the world. The boys ate slowly at first, then faster once they realized there was plenty. Cole talked across the table about practice and a play they had run earlier.

Marcus mostly listened.

After dinner Megan packed a small bag at the counter.

Bread. Peanut butter. A few things from the pantry. More food than Marcus had seen in his kitchen in weeks.

She handed it to him casually.

"Just some extra."

Marcus nodded. "Thank you, ma'am."

He meant it more than he could explain.

• • •

That night Marcus lay on the mattress staring at the ceiling.

He should have felt lucky.
He knew that.

But another thought pressed into his mind anyway.
He did not want to be the kid people felt sorry for.

Because once people started seeing you that way, they stopped expecting anything from you.

On the field nobody looked at him like that. Nobody asked about his kitchen or what was missing from his refrigerator. They just expected him to run the route correctly and catch the ball.
At that table tonight they had looked at him differently.

Not in a bad way.

Just in a way that made him feel smaller than he wanted to be.

Marcus turned onto his side and pulled the blanket tighter around his shoulders. He thought about the field. The lights. The sound of cleats cutting into turf.

He thought about the way Coach Mercer listened more than he talked.

Practice was not just where he played football.

It was where the world slowed down long enough for him to breathe.

Marcus closed his eyes.

Tomorrow morning he would make the sandwiches again. Tomorrow he would get on the bus. Tomorrow he would stay after practice.

Not because he had to.

Because it was the one place he wanted to be.

CHAPTER SIX

When Belief Divides

Present Day

The staff meeting felt different the moment Jack walked in.

Not loud. Not hostile. Just tired, like something had been drained from the room, and no one wanted to say what it was.

Sunday afternoons had always been predictable here. Film already cued up. Coffee reheated. Folding chairs were pulled closer together than they had been on Saturday mornings. This was where weekends officially ended, where games got dissected, and fixes were supposed to begin.

The whiteboard was already filled. Formations sketched in dry-erase. Install notes left over from the last meeting. Run fits circled, coverage checks underlined. Someone had drawn a new blitz package in the corner, half-finished but hopeful.

The staff had come ready to talk football.

Jack didn't erase any of it.

"We're not where we need to be," Jack said. "But we're moving."

A chair shifted. Someone clicked a pen. The film paused on the screen behind him.

An assistant cleared his throat. "Some of this beyond-the-game stuff," he said carefully. "It's fine. I get it. But football still wins games, and we haven't won any yet. Nobody wants to hear that when we are losing."

Jack nodded. "You're right."

The assistant relaxed. A few others did too. This was the turn they expected. Adjustments. Tweaks. Something that could be fixed by Tuesday.

"Football wins games," Jack repeated. "But this stuff keeps kids from quitting when they're tired, scared, or losing."

The room went still.

That hadn't been on the board.

Ray Holloway leaned back against the wall, arms crossed. He wasn't posturing. He never did. Ray had been in this room for over twenty years. On Sunday afternoons after blowouts, Sunday afternoons after the few wins, and Sundays when the tape felt heavier than the score.

Ray believed in football. In preparation. In doing things the right way. Jack knew that. He respected it.

"If you're changing things, we might want to start with how to tackle and block better," Ray said.

There was no hard edge in it. Just concern.

"Yes," Jack replied. "I am. We need to get better at football, but first we need to get better as men."

Ray nodded slowly, eyes drifting back to the board. The plays. The notes. The work that had always been the answer here.

"Just make sure we don't forget what wins," Ray said.

Jack felt the pull of it. The simplicity. The comfort of fixing problems with diagrams and installs, trusting that effort would carry the rest. Ray wasn't wrong about football.

Jack knew that.

That was the problem.

"I won't," Jack said. "But I'm not pretending it's enough anymore; we have got to find a way to get them to see their potential in more than just football."

"Kids need clear lines, Coach," Ray said. "Not just words on a board. I've seen belief without discipline turn into excuses."

No one spoke.

This wasn't an argument.

It was a line being redrawn.

Jack dismissed the meeting.

Chairs scraped back. The room emptied in pieces. Conversations cut short. Eyes avoided his.

Jack noticed who stayed.
He noticed who left immediately.

One chair scraped back louder than the rest. That was the coach Jack had expected to stay.

He didn't.

That line was becoming clearer every week.

The last of the staff drifted out, chairs scraping softly as they went. The room settled into that familiar quiet that only came after everyone else had left.

• • •

Jack gathered a few papers on the desk, not in any hurry.

He heard the door close again.

Coach Evans was still there.

Evans leaned against the wall for a moment, hands in his pockets, like he wasn't sure whether to speak or leave.

"Something on your mind?" Jack asked.

Evans nodded once. "Yeah. I guess there is."

Jack waited.

Evans glanced toward the door, then back at him. "I want you to know… I believe in what you're trying to do here."

Jack didn't answer right away. He just nodded slightly, letting Evans keep talking.

"But," Evans continued, "not everybody does."

Jack leaned back against the desk. "I figured."

Evans gave a short, quiet smile. "It's not personal. It's just… they've seen a lot of coaches come through here. Every one of them had a plan. Every one of them was sure this was the thing that would fix it."

He paused.

"And none of it ever lasted."

The words weren't sharp. Just honest.

"They're not against you," Evans said. "They're protecting themselves from believing again."

Jack looked down at the practice field through the office window, lights still on, the yard lines glowing pale in the dark.

"That makes sense," he said.

Evans shifted his weight. "I've been here long enough to know the difference between noise and steadiness. And you've been steady."

Jack didn't respond.

"Eleven straight losses," Evans went on quietly. "Most guys would've started changing everything by now. Talking louder. Coaching harder. Trying to prove something."

He shook his head slightly.

"You didn't."

Jack exhaled slowly. "Panicking doesn't fix anything."

"No," Evans said. "It doesn't."

They stood there a moment, both looking through the window, out at the empty field.

Evans finally pushed off the wall. "Just thought you should know that not everybody's doubting."

"I appreciate that," Jack said.

Evans nodded once and headed for the door.

When it closed behind him, the room felt quiet again—but not the same kind of quiet as before.

Jack stood there a moment longer, looking out at the field.

Belief didn't arrive all at once.

Sometimes it showed up one person at a time.

Jack understood something then that no coaching clinic ever taught him.

Culture change costs people.

Last year, he'd known what needed to change and still backed away from it. He'd hidden behind the installs and terminology. Let the staff argue scheme because it felt safer than forcing alignment.

Keep it just about football, and everyone understands. Make it about more than that, and people become uncomfortable.

Maybe belief was overrated. Maybe effort and execution were enough.

He'd told himself that once.

Now he wasn't so sure.

They had worked. They had prepared. They knew their assignments. He had completely focused on scheme.

And they still lost.

Jack felt the weight of it settle. Not confidence. Resolve.

He knew what came next. Some would leave quietly. Others would stay just long enough to see if he blinked.

He didn't resent them for it. He wondered if he was wrong. If all of this mattered when the lights came on.

Then he decided it had to.

He wouldn't chase them.
Not now.
Not from the bottom.

And not everyone was willing to stay long enough to find out.

CHAPTER SEVEN

27 and Counting

The number wasn't written anywhere in the locker room.

Nobody posted it on a board. Nobody mentioned it in meetings. Nobody used it in a speech.

But everyone knew it.

Twenty-seven.

Twenty-seven varsity games without a win.

It sat in the room with them when they dressed.
It followed them onto the practice field.
It rode home with them on buses where nobody talked much anymore.

No one said it out loud, but everyone carried it.

Friday night came anyway.

The opponent wasn't West Ridge.
Wasn't River Bend.

Wasn't a team anyone would have circled on a calendar.

It was Riverview, a team Iron Valley should have beaten the year before. They even led for most of the game, but found a way to lose at the end.

Everyone in the county knew it. The players knew it. The parents knew it. Even the opposing fans knew it.

That was what made it dangerous.

Games you're supposed to win carry a different kind of weight. Not fear of losing to someone better, but fear of proving nothing has changed.

Warm-ups were quiet. Not tense. Just focused. Helmets went on earlier than usual. Conversations stayed short.

Jack watched it from the sideline and said nothing.
They were learning.

The first quarter was ugly.

Two penalties stalled drives. A missed tackle extended a possession that should have ended. A dropped pass killed field position. The crowd shifted restlessly, like people bracing for something familiar.

Jack felt it too, that old pull of doubt. Not loud. Just there, waiting.

But something was different.

No one panicked.
No one hung their heads.
They lined up again.

Late in the second quarter, something finally settled.

Tyler Briggs caved the right side of the line on an inside zone. Cole pressed the hole, cut once, and got north. Twelve yards. Then eight more. Then five.

Nothing explosive.
Just steady.

Three plays later, Cole followed Tyler again and crossed the goal line untouched.

7–0.

The sideline didn't erupt.
It exhaled.

At halftime, the locker room was quiet—not discouraged, not confident. Just steady.

Jack didn't give a speech.

"Keep doing what you're doing," he said. "Nothing fancy. Nothing different."

They nodded.
That was enough.

The third quarter felt longer than it was.

Marcus started finding space. Not big plays—chains-moving plays. Routes finished. Hands strong. Eyes calm. Cole began to settle into the rhythm of the game, no longer rushing reads, no longer pressing.

Midway through the third quarter, Iron Valley drove again.
Tyler finished a block that turned four yards into nine.

Marcus converted a third down with a catch in traffic. Cole kept the ball on a read and slipped past a linebacker who hesitated just long enough.

Touchdown.
14–0.

For a moment, the stadium didn't know how to react.

Then the noise came, loud, relieved, almost disbelieving.

On the kickoff that followed, Neil Parker sprinted downfield and met the returner at the twenty-five.

Clean hit. Solo tackle.

He got up fast, looking around like he wasn't sure whether to celebrate or jog back to the sideline. Tyler slapped his helmet as he passed. Marcus pointed at him. Neil tried not to smile and failed.

Jack noticed.

The fourth quarter reminded them how far they still had to go.

The first turnover came on a strip sack.

Cole stepped up, eyes downfield, trying to let the concept finish. The protection held—almost. Then the edge collapsed, and a helmet found the ball. It wasn't a violent hit; it was just precise. The kind defenders practice. The ball flew loose and skipped along the turf, end over end, as linemen dove and reached and missed by inches. Someone screamed "BALL!" like yelling could change physics.

It didn't.
Their guy fell on it first.

The second came on a tipped pass.

Cole threw a quick hitch, trying to calm the moment, trying to get them back into rhythm. A hand flashed up in the throwing lane, and the ball popped straight into the air like a coin toss. Jack watched it spin under the lights, slow enough to feel cruel. The defender caught it at shoulder height and cradled it like it was the easiest thing he'd done all night.

The third was a fumbled exchange that bounced the wrong way.

The mesh point was supposed to be automatic. Cole's eyes on the end. The back's eyes on the track. For one beat, it looked normal, but then the ball slid, clipped a hip, and hit the ground with a hollow thud.

Both of them reached for it.

Both of them were a step late. The ball took a hard kick off the turf and rolled straight into open space—right where the other team was waiting.

Jack grabbed Cole by the shoulder as he came off the field.
"Ball security," Jack said quietly.

Cole nodded, breathing hard. "Yes, sir."

Cole sat at the end of the bench, helmet still on, chinstrap hanging loose.

He wasn't watching the field.

He was staring at the turf between his cleats.

Jack walked past and heard him mutter, barely above a whisper.

"I'm trying."

Not to anyone.
Just to himself.

Jack kept walking, because sometimes the hardest part of being a father was pretending to be only a coach.

Each time, the defense held, but barely. Pads cracked louder now. Pursuit angles shortened. Tackles finished with a little more urgency than they had in the first half. The sideline stopped talking and started watching.

In the stands, the noise changed. It wasn't cheering anymore. It was counting. Counting down and distance, counting the seconds between plays, and counting the slow crawl of the clock.

Everyone could feel it tightening.

With four minutes left, the other team finally broke through.
14–7.

The kickoff sailed deep. Iron Valley ran three plays and punted.

Not again was creeping into Jack's mind. Into every player's mind.
One last drive.

Jack stood with his headset resting crooked on one ear, eyes fixed on the field, hands buried in his pockets. He didn't pace. Didn't shout. He just watched.

The ball was on the opponent's own thirty-five. Iron Valley's defense had to protect a late lead. Everyone on the sideline understood what that meant.

The first play went for five. A simple run, nothing fancy, just enough to stay on schedule.

Second down. Another run, pushing the pile forward for three more.

Third and two.

The crowd leaned forward. Iron Valley crowded the line, safeties creeping down, everyone knowing what was coming. The snap came, and the back bounced outside just before contact, slipping past a reaching arm and falling ahead for four.

First down.

Jack exhaled slowly through his nose and shifted his weight, eyes never leaving the field.

At midfield now. A short pass moved the chains again, the receiver catching it in traffic, spinning upfield, and racing down the sideline to the 28-yard line.

Two minutes left on the clock.

Another third-down conversion.

The defense jogged back to the line, hands on hips, breathing heavier now. No one looked at the sideline. They just reset.

Another run. Six yards. Then three more.

Third and one. One minute left on the clock.

The ball was on the twenty now. The offense lined up quickly as they hurried to get the first down.

The snap came.

Tyler read it immediately.

The guard pulled late and Tyler shot through the crease, shedding the block with his inside shoulder and meeting the back in the hole. The collision popped in the air, pads cracking, both players stumbling forward but falling short.

Fourth and four. Timeout. Forty-two seconds left.

Quick adjustments from Coach Holloway.

Jack leaned slightly forward, hands still in his pockets, saying nothing. Around him, the sideline had gone quiet, not tense, not frantic, just locked in.

They had seen this show last year a few times and not been able to make the stop.

The offense broke the huddle and came to the line.

The quarterback stepped to the line, scanning. The receivers split wide.

The snap came clean. The quarterback dropped, looking left first, then back across the middle. The pocket held for a moment, then began to tighten. He slid once and fired toward a receiver breaking inside the sticks.

Then, the ball hit the turf a step in front of him.

Incomplete.

For half a second, the stadium didn't react, like it needed confirmation.

Then the whistle came.

Iron Valley's sideline and crowd exploded.

They had bent.

But they hadn't broken.

Cole brought the offense on the field in victory formation for one more play.

The horn sounded.

For a second, no one moved. The seniors looked at each other, confirming this was real.

Then it hit again.

Not just a roar.
A release.

Helmets went up. Players grabbed each other. A few jumped. A few just stood there, breathing hard, like they weren't sure it was real yet.

Jack turned toward the sideline and saw Tyler Briggs.

Tyler wasn't yelling.

He was crying.

Not hiding it. Not wiping it away. Just standing there, helmet in one hand, tears running down a face that had taken more losses than most kids ever should.

A couple of the other seniors stood nearby, eyes red, jaws tight, shoulders shaking as they tried to laugh it off.

Twenty-seven games.
Jack stepped towards Tyler.

Tyler was still holding his helmet, staring out at the field like he wasn't ready to leave it yet.

"Hey," Jack said quietly.

Tyler wiped his face with the back of his wrist, embarrassed for a second, then shook his head.

"Sorry, Coach," he said. "I didn't think we'd ever…"
He stopped, swallowing.

Jack shook his head. "Don't apologize."

Tyler looked back at the field. "I wasn't sure it was ever going to happen," he said. Not dramatic. Just honest.

Jack didn't answer right away. He followed Tyler's eyes across the field, to the empty end zone, the hash marks, the place where so many Friday nights had ended the wrong way.

"It happened," Jack said.

Tyler nodded once, slow, like he was committing it to memory.

For a second neither of them moved.

Then Tyler stepped forward and wrapped his arms around Jack in a quick, tight hug, the kind players give when there aren't words that fit.

Jack returned it, just as briefly, a hand on the back of Tyler's shoulder pads.

"Proud of you," Jack said quietly.

Tyler nodded again, eyes still red, then pulled his helmet back on and jogged toward his teammates.

Jack watched him go, realizing something he hadn't fully understood before.

Wins don't mean the same thing to everyone.

Some players celebrate.
Some players heal.

Jack felt something in his chest shift.

He had started to think about the turnovers. The penalties. The missed fits. All the things that still weren't good enough.

Then he looked at those seniors again. And he let it go.

Parents were already spilling down from the stands. Administrators shaking hands. Cameras out. Smiles everywhere.

Jack usually stayed guarded in moments like this. Careful. Measured. Already thinking about Monday.

But then he saw Megan.

She was standing near the fence, talking with a couple of parents, smiling in a way he hadn't seen in a while, not polite, not supportive.

Proud.

Jack let himself feel it then.

Just for a moment.
Not the relief of winning.
The relief of seeing people believe again.

• • •

Later that night, the house filled up.

Cleats by the door. Plates in hands. Laughter in the living room. Kids sitting on the floor, leaning against walls, talking about plays like they'd been part of something bigger than themselves.

Neil sat on the edge of the couch, still replaying his tackle in quiet conversation with Marcus. Tyler ate slowly, quieter than usual, but lighter somehow. Cole leaned back against the wall, tired but relaxed in a way Jack hadn't seen in a long time.

Jack stood in the kitchen, watching it.

Megan came up beside him.

"They needed that," she said.

Jack nodded.

"So did you," she added.

Jack looked around the room again, at the noise, the life, the belief starting to breathe.

"Yeah," he said quietly. "We did."

Outside, the night was still. The stadium lights had long gone dark.

But something had changed.
Not everything.
But something.

And for the first time in a long time, Iron Valley wasn't counting losses anymore.

They were counting forward.

CHAPTER EIGHT

Tyler

Tyler didn't leave Coach Mercer's house until most of the others were gone.

The noise had faded to small conversations. A few kids still sat on the floor, replaying plays that already felt bigger in memory than they had on the field. Someone laughed in the kitchen. Plates clinked. The kind of sound that only came after a win.

Tyler stood near the door for a minute before stepping outside.

The night air felt cool against his face. The adrenaline was still there, humming in his chest, but it wasn't as sharp as it had been an hour earlier. It was starting to settle into something slower.

Something heavier.

He drove home with the windows down, the road quiet, the town already asleep. A few porch lights were still on. A dog barked somewhere in the distance. The world felt normal again in a way that almost surprised him.

Like the game hadn't just happened.

Like twenty-seven losses hadn't just ended.

When he pulled into the driveway, the kitchen light was still on.

His mom was sitting at the table, still in her work clothes, a mug in her hands.

She looked up when he walked in.

"There he is," she said.

Tyler nodded, setting his keys on the counter.

"I'm sorry I couldn't be there," she said. "They needed me to stay late."

"It's okay," Tyler said. And he meant it.

She studied him for a moment, then smiled.

"I'm proud of you," she said.

The words landed harder than he expected.

Tyler looked down, rubbing the back of his neck. "We all played good."

"I know," she said. "But I'm proud of you."

He nodded once, not trusting himself to say much.

They sat in the quiet for a moment, the refrigerator humming softly, the house settling around them.

"You hungry?" she asked.

"Nah," Tyler said. "Still full."

"That's good," she said, standing and rinsing her mug. "Get some sleep. Long week ahead."

"Yeah."

Tyler headed down the hallway to his room.

When he sat on the edge of the bed, the adrenaline finally started to drain out of him. His legs felt heavy. His shoulders ached in that deep, satisfying way that only came after a game.

For a while, he just sat there, staring at nothing, letting the quiet settle.

And then, without warning, the memories came back.

Not the good ones.

The ones that stayed.

• • •

Sophomore Year

The lights were brighter then.

Or maybe he just remembered them that way.

The game was tied late in the fourth quarter. The air was cold enough that every breath stung a little. Tyler crouched at the line, hands on his thighs, trying to slow his breathing.

Just one drive, he remembered thinking. Just one.

The ball was snapped.

The play broke outside, their back cutting upfield, the sideline already erupting as he crossed the goal line.

Touchdown.

For one second, Tyler felt nothing but relief.

Then he saw the flag.

Yellow on the turf.

Holding.

The noise in the stadium changed instantly. The cheer collapsed into groans and scattered shouting. Teammates slowed. The back jogged toward the sideline, not looking at anyone.

Tyler didn't need to ask.

He knew.

The walk back to the sideline felt longer than the entire drive.

The coach met him near the numbers.

"What are you doing?" the coach snapped, loud enough that players turned. "You just cost us the game."

Tyler stared at the ground.

The coach kept talking. Not correcting. Not teaching. Just talking, voice sharp, words landing harder than the hit Tyler had taken on the play.

Players heard it.
Parents heard it.
Everyone heard it.

Tyler wished the ground would open up and take him with it.

The drive stalled two plays later.

They lost by three.

From then on, every loss felt personal to Tyler.

• • •

Later That Night

The house smelled like cigarette smoke and leftover dinner.

His dad sat at the kitchen table, a game replay flickering on the television.

"You see that?" his dad said, not looking at him. "That's the kind of thing that gets coaches fired. Those morons can't call a good game if their life depended on it."

Tyler stood there, still in his jacket.

"They don't care about you," his dad said. "That program's been bad for years. They suck and will always suck."

He leaned back in his chair.

"Why keep going? There is no reason to stay on that team."

Tyler didn't answer.

He didn't know how to explain something he didn't understand himself.

He just went to his room and sat on the edge of the bed, staring at the wall, the sound of the television drifting down the hallway.

• • •

One Year Later

He woke up, and the house felt different.

Not just quieter.

Empty.

His dad's boots weren't by the door and his truck wasn't in the driveway.

His mom moved around the kitchen slowly, not saying much.

"Where's Dad?" Tyler asked.

She hesitated.

"He's gone for a while," she said.

Tyler nodded.

He didn't ask where.

After a few days, he stopped expecting to hear the truck in the driveway at night.

But the football field was always there for him.

• • •

Present

Tyler blinked, the dark of his room coming back into focus.

A short text from a teammate still fired up over the win.

The ceiling fan turned slowly overhead.

The house was quiet again, but it was a different quiet now.

Not empty.

Just still.

He lay back on the bed, staring at the ceiling, feeling the last of the adrenaline fade out of his body.

For a long time, staying had felt like stubbornness.

Showing up when the score didn't matter.
Lifting when nobody believed it would change anything.
Playing for a program everyone else had already given up on.

But tonight felt different.

Tonight, for the first time, staying felt like it meant something.

Tyler closed his eyes.

And for the first time in a long time, he slept without replaying a loss in his head.

CHAPTER NINE

Winning Changes the Argument

The win didn't change the room, but it rearranged it.

Sunday's staff meeting started differently. Coffee cups were fuller. Someone made a weak joke about finally getting the taste out of their mouth. A couple of assistants laughed—short, surprised, like they weren't used to hearing themselves do it.

Movement and conversations picked up.

After they had met in smaller groups, Jack stood at the front, arms folded, watching the room settle. The film wasn't even on yet.

He let the quiet stretch a beat longer than normal.

"Good job Friday," he said. No volume.

A few heads nodded. A little celebration clap. It died down quickly, and when it did, Ray finally spoke.

"We left points out there."

Jack nodded. "We did."

Silence settled again.

Jack picked up a marker but didn't write anything. The faint outline of this week's word—**TRUST**—already on the board.

"We celebrate effort," Jack said. "We correct execution. We don't worship outcomes."

Someone muttered, "Tell that to the crowd."
A few coaches smirked.

Jack didn't respond.

He capped the marker and set it down.

"Get with your coordinators and finish up what you've been working on. We will continue using our themes for the week. That's all for today," he said.

The meeting ended more quickly than usual. Chairs slid back.

Conversations stayed low. A couple of assistants lingered to gather papers, then drifted out.

Ray didn't move.

• • •

When the door shut, the room felt different.

Ray stood near the board, staring at the faint word still visible.

"Kids played hard Friday," he said.

"They did," Jack answered.

Ray nodded once, slowly. "But hard isn't what wins in this league."

Jack didn't respond.

Ray turned toward him. "You know that."

"I do."

"Then why does it feel like we're talking about everything but football in meetings? You've asked me to scale back on our defense to the point of boredom for me."

Jack leaned back against his desk, arms folded, not defensive, just tired.

"Because football wasn't the problem last year," he said. "You have a great system on defense, and we are solid in scheme. We worked. We practiced. We installed. And we still lost. Our kids need to be able to understand what we are asking from them and believe in it."

Ray shook his head. "We didn't execute."

Jack nodded. "That's part of it."

"Most of it," Ray said.

Silence sat between them.

Jack looked down at the notebook on his desk, then back up.

"Winning is a byproduct," he said quietly. "Of habits. Of standards. Of belief. You know that as well as I do."

Ray didn't answer right away.

When he finally spoke, his voice was quieter.

"I've watched this place lose for a long time," he said. "I've watched good coaches come through here and get run off because people wanted something different instead of something better."

Jack listened.
Ray's eyes moved around the room, at the photos, plaques, and years of seasons stacked in frames.

"I don't want to watch it happen again," Ray said.

Jack nodded slowly. "Neither do I."

Ray studied him. "Then don't forget what matters."

Jack met his eyes. "I'm trying to build a program that lasts."

Neither man spoke after that.

The silence didn't feel angry.

It felt final.

Ray picked up his notebook and left without another word.

Jack stood alone in the room for a while, staring at the board, at the faint outline of TRUST fading under the lights.

He had known Ray was frustrated, but had hoped they could coexist as they built something together. Now he was not sure.

• • •

Monday felt different.

The locker room buzzed in a way it hadn't before. Laughter lingered. The music played a little louder. Kids walked taller, like the weight they'd been carrying had shifted just enough to let them breathe.

Jack noticed who was watching him when he walked in.

Not nervously.
Curiously.

A senior finally asked it.

"Coach… you don't look happy."

Jack leaned against the wall.

"I am," he said. "But I'm careful."

The room quieted.

He looked at Tyler, then Marcus, then the rest.

"Winning is great, but it is just a part of our goals," Jack said. "We want to do things the right way and let winning take care of itself."

He let it sit.

"Football will end. Life doesn't care what the record was when that happens. My job is to prepare you for that moment."

Silence held.

"We want to keep pushing you to be ready for what comes after."

No one clapped.
They didn't need to.

• • •

Monday afternoon, Marcus Reed stayed late.

Still trying to get better.

He didn't ask permission. Didn't announce it. Just stayed again running routes, catching balls, repeating footwork until the sun dipped low.

Coach Evans stayed too.

Evans corrected quietly. No speeches. Just teaching.

Marcus laughed once. A real laugh.

Jack filed it away. It was good to find a place where Marcus could be a kid.

Trust didn't arrive all at once.
It leaked in slowly.

• • •

Tuesday at practice, Marcus was late.
Ten minutes.

Nothing dramatic.

But late.

Jack met him at the door.

"Locker room," Jack said.

Marcus nodded and went.

He sat on the bench, hands clasped, waiting.

Jack stepped inside.

"Standard hasn't changed."

Marcus nodded. "I know."

"Sit today."

Marcus swallowed. "Yes, sir."

He sat, eyes on the floor, shoulders tight.

Word spread fast.
Some assistants approved. Others didn't.
Jack remembered the empty locker two seasons ago.

He hadn't forgotten what that cost. This time, the kid was still here.

That afternoon, Marcus sat on the bleachers while practice ran. Evans sat beside him.
Marcus nodded while Evans talked, but inside he felt heat rising.

He'd sat.
He'd taken it.
He hadn't argued.

But part of him wanted to.

Part of him wanted to say that some kids had rides waiting.
Some kids had lights on at home.
Some kids didn't have to think about food before practice.

He didn't say any of it.

But the thought stayed with him longer than he liked.

After practice, Jack found him near the fence.

"You okay?" Jack asked.

Marcus hesitated. "You're not done with me? I heard about Evan. I don't want to be off the team."

Jack shook his head. "Not even close. Run your punishment tomorrow and don't be late again."

Marcus exhaled like he'd been holding his breath for weeks.

• • •

That night, Jack sat alone at the kitchen table.

A notebook lay open in front of him.

The next theme word sat half-written, the ink darker where the pen had paused.

Wins made people louder.
Standards made them quieter.

Jack stared at the page a moment longer.

He thought about the empty locker from two seasons ago. The standard had been clear. Late and miss the game.

He just hadn't looked closely enough at the kid standing in front of him. Sometimes fair is not equal, and that was what made his job so hard.

This time, he had, and the kid stayed.

Did the team need him to uphold more standards or more compassion?

Jack rubbed his eyes and leaned back in the chair, staring at the ceiling.

He wasn't sure yet which one the program needed more of.

And he wasn't sure which one would cost him more to hold onto.

The house was quiet.

For now, that was enough.

CHAPTER TEN

Some Lines Don't Bend

The meeting request came first thing in the morning.

No subject line.
No urgency.
Just a calendar block from administration.

Jack knew.

He didn't rush. He finished the film. Answered two players' texts. Walked the hallway once before heading down. The office lights were already on when he arrived.

Jack stepped into the hallway.

Ray sat on the bench outside the office, elbows on his knees, staring at the floor.

He didn't look up when the door opened.

Jack paused for a second, then kept walking.

Ray still didn't look up.

Jack stepped into the office.

The room felt different from the field house. Cleaner. Quieter. The kind of quiet that came from closed doors and carpet instead of whistles and cleats.

Three administrators sat around the small conference table. Coffee cups rested in front of them, untouched, and a legal pad lay open in front of the principal with the pen placed neatly across the top like it had been arranged instead of used. The wall clock ticked once behind them.

Jack took the empty chair. No one spoke right away.

Finally, the principal cleared his throat.

"We've had a few concerns brought to us," he said. Not accusatory. Just careful.

Jack nodded.

The athletic director leaned back slightly in his chair. "Mostly about discipline," he said. "Some parents feel like standards are… uneven."

Jack didn't respond.

The assistant principal adjusted a paperweight on the table before speaking. "And accountability," she added. "There's a perception that some players are being treated differently."

Perception.

Jack heard the word and understood what it meant. Someone had been talking. Probably more than one someone.

The principal folded his hands. "Jack, we're not saying you're wrong," he said. "We're saying the perception is becoming a distraction."

The clock ticked again.

Jack let the silence sit. He had been in rooms like this before; rooms where nobody raised their voice, where no one said exactly what they meant, but the meaning was clear anyway.

"And culture," the principal said carefully. "We just want to make sure the focus stays on football."

Jack waited a moment before answering.

"It is," he said simply.

Another pause followed. No one argued. No one pushed. They weren't accusing him of anything he could defend against. They were reminding him who was watching.

Jack listened while they spoke a little longer, concerns phrased as questions, worries disguised as suggestions. He didn't interrupt. Didn't explain.

He had learned a long time ago that explanations in rooms like this rarely changed minds.

Results did.

Eventually, the principal closed the folder in front of him.

"That's all we wanted to discuss," he said.

Chairs shifted quietly as the meeting broke apart. Jack stood.

"I'll handle it," he said.

They nodded, relieved. Not because the problem was solved, but because it now belonged to someone else.

Jack stepped back into the hallway and paused for a moment before heading toward the field house.

Pressure didn't always shout.

Sometimes it wore a tie and thanked you for coming in.

Ray followed him back down the hallway, silent until they reached Jack's office.

Jack shut the door.

Ray stayed standing.

"So," Ray said. "This is about Marcus."

"It's about direction," Jack replied.

Ray exhaled sharply. "You're letting emotion run the program."

Jack leaned back against his desk. "I'm letting people run it. Standards without compassion don't work."

Ray shook his head. "Standards mean consequences."

"They do," Jack said. "That's why I enforced them."

"Not enough," Ray snapped. "That kid's late, he should sit. Period."

Jack met his eyes. "He did sit."

Ray scoffed. "Not when it matters."

"That's where we differ," Jack said calmly. "Practice always matters."

Ray laughed once, bitterly. "You're changing the rules now."

Jack nodded. "I am."

Silence stretched between them.

"I've been here twenty-two years," Ray said finally. "I've seen what works and what doesn't work."

Jack didn't argue.

"I know you have," he said. "And I respect it."

Ray's eyes narrowed. "That doesn't sound like respect."

"It is," Jack replied. "It's just not agreement."

Ray stepped closer. "You're losing the locker room. This will not end well."

Jack didn't flinch. "No. I'm losing the ones who only trusted in what we are doing when it is easy."

Ray stared at him.

That was the moment.

Not anger.
Not betrayal.
Recognition.

"You don't trust me," Ray said quietly.

Jack shook his head. "I don't trust the direction you want to take us."

Ray swallowed. "So that's it."

Jack nodded. "I can't ask these kids to buy into something I don't fully believe in. I want you here, but you have to be on board with where I want to go."

Ray looked around the office, the photos on the wall, playbooks stacked on the desk, a season still unfinished.

He made his decision.

"You'll regret this," Ray said.

Jack held his gaze. "Maybe."

Ray grabbed his jacket.

At the door, he stopped.

"You think being a friend to them makes you strong," Ray said. "Sometimes it just makes you soft."

Jack answered without hesitation.

"I think we are called to do what is best for each kid, and it may look different."

Ray didn't respond.

He left.

Jack stood there a moment after the door closed.

Through the office window, he could see Ray crossing the parking lot, shoulders stiff against the cold morning air.

Twenty-two years of Iron Valley football walked out that door with him.

• • •

The kitchen bulb threw long shadows across the table. Jack's coffee sat untouched, steam curling up and disappearing.

His right thumb traced the same groove in the wood grain over and over, wearing it a little deeper. Megan set her mug down without a sound. When she finally spoke, her voice was softer than the hum of the refrigerator.

"You okay?"

Jack's head moved once, half nod, half surrender. His eyes stayed on the dark window where his reflection stared back, older than he remembered.

She waited.

"He wasn't wrong about everything," Jack said finally. "That's the part that hurts."

Megan reached across the table and rested her hand on his.

"He's been here a long time," she said quietly.

Jack nodded.

"Sometimes people who've been somewhere the longest," she continued, "are the ones who struggle most when it changes."

Jack exhaled slowly. "Why do I feel so conflicted? I know this was the right thing for Marcus and our team."

"Doing the right thing doesn't always feel great," she added.

Jack leaned back, staring at the ceiling.

Leadership, he realized, wasn't about winning arguments. It was about choosing which ones you were willing to lose.

And he had just lost the one assistant who still remembered every losing season by name—the one who could spot a missed gap from the press box before the whistle.

Ray wasn't a bad guy. And losing experienced coaches hurt more than Jack wanted to admit. But for this to work, everyone had to be on board with the direction he was taking them.

And the direction was clear now.

For the first time since that opening night—
Jack didn't doubt it.

And Friday was coming fast.

Getting ready for the next week was going to be a chore already after the emotional high of the first win.

And now, missing Ray would be a bigger challenge.

CHAPTER ELEVEN

When Belief Has to Breathe

Practice ended on a long whistle.

Helmets came off. Players drifted toward the sideline in small groups, breathing hard, pads popping softly as shoulder straps loosened.

It had been a good practice.

Clean. Focused.

But quieter than usual.

Jack stood near the numbers, watching the last drill group jog in. He felt it again, that space on the defensive side where Ray used to stand. Nobody barking reminders between reps. Nobody catching small alignment mistakes before the snap.

Just a little more silence than there used to be.

A sophomore linebacker lingered nearby, turning his mouthpiece in his fingers.

"Coach?" he said.

Jack looked over. "Yeah."

The kid hesitated, then asked, "Is Coach Holloway coming back?"

Jack didn't answer right away.

A few players slowed as they walked past, not stopping, but not hurrying either.

"No," Jack said finally.

The kid nodded, eyes dropping to the turf.

"He was hard on us," the player said. "But… he made us better."

Jack felt that land deeper than the kid probably intended.

"I know," Jack said quietly.

The kid nodded once and jogged toward the locker room.

Jack watched him go.

Around him, the field settled into evening—the sound of cleats fading, the equipment cart rattling toward the shed, the wind pushing lightly across the empty grass.

Practice had gone well.

It still felt like something was missing.

• • •

Thursday's practice was running long.

Inside run drill had gone an extra ten minutes, and the air felt heavier than it had at the start. Helmets were damp, voices quieter between reps, the rhythm of practice settling into that tired, steady grind that came near the end of the day.

Marcus jogged out of a rep and glanced toward the clock on the scoreboard.

Then again.

On the next whistle, he stepped toward the sideline and caught Jack's eye.

"Coach," Marcus said, breathing hard. "I gotta leave right after stretch."

Jack looked at him. "Everything alright?"

"Yes, sir," Marcus said. "I just need to pick up my brother from his practice."

Jack nodded once. "Go ahead when we break."

Marcus didn't say anything else. Just nodded and jogged back into the drill.

Practice ended ten minutes later.

While most of the players lingered, helmets off, talking, dragging their feet toward the locker room, Marcus was already grabbing his bag, pulling his cleats loose as he walked.

Cole caught him near the gate.

"You heading out?" Cole asked.

Marcus nodded. "Gotta get Dylan."

Cole watched him jog toward the parking lot, bag slung over one shoulder, moving fast but not hurried, the way someone moved when this wasn't unusual, just part of the day.

Cole stood there a second longer, then turned back toward the locker room.

Inside, the noise of the team carried on like always.

But for some of them, responsibility didn't end at the whistle.

• • •

The next opponent didn't care about Iron Valley's first win.

They hadn't watched the tears.
Hadn't felt the release.
Hadn't sat in a locker room where winning meant survival.

Didn't care that they had lost a coach.

Pine Bluff came in undefeated.

Big up front. Quarterback with offers. A defense that played fast and talked faster. The kind of team Iron Valley had lost to for years and then explained away on Saturday mornings.

"This one will tell us something," Jack told the staff during the week.

He didn't say what.

Friday night told it for him.

Iron Valley fell behind early.

On the first defensive series, Pine Bluff lined up in a formation Iron Valley had seen on film. Tight end motioned across, pulling the strong safety wide and leaving the B gap soft. It was the kind of pre-snap tell Ray Holloway used to catch from the press box before the ball was even snapped. He'd key the headset twice and say, "Watch the motion, they're coming backside."

Nobody keyed the headset.

Evans was up there now, doing his best, but he was learning the view from the press box the same week he was learning to call a defense on his own. The back hit the B gap untouched. Forty-two yards. Touchdown.

Jack pulled his headset off for a second and pressed his thumb hard against the bridge of his nose. He wanted to say something sharp into the mic. Something about seeing the motion. About adjusting pre-snap. About twenty-two years of experience walking out the door and nobody filling the gap it left.

He didn't say it.

He put the headset back on and said, "Check the motion next time. They'll run it again."

Evans's voice came back steady. "Got it, Coach."

But the frustration sat in Jack's chest like a weight. Not at Evans. Evans was doing everything he could. The frustration was at himself, for making a decision he still believed was right and watching it cost them in real time on a Friday night.

Turnover on the next possession. Short field. Another score.

14–0 before Iron Valley had found its footing.

Jack didn't panic.

But he felt the old pressure crawl up his spine. The one that whispered, *Here it is. This is where it breaks.*

The crowd grew restless. Murmurs instead of cheers. A few hands went to pockets.

Cole pressed early and tried to make something happen instead of letting it come. Marcus got bracketed. The run game stalled.

By halftime, Iron Valley trailed 21–7.

The locker room was quiet, but not hollow.

Jack looked at their faces. Nobody quit. Nobody checked out.

"We don't need everything," Jack said. "We need the next play."

That's when Tyler Briggs spoke up.

Senior guard. Team captain. Thick through the shoulders. Quiet in meetings. Loud between the lines. Tyler had never once pointed a finger.

"Coach," Tyler said, voice steady, "they're tired."

A few heads turned.

"They're playing soft," Tyler added. "We're playing pretty football and trying to be cute. Let us lean on them and stop trying to trick them."

Jack met his eyes.

Tyler didn't flinch.

"Alright," Jack said. "Let's go to work."

The third quarter didn't look like a comeback.

Iron Valley traded punts. Took shots. Took hits. Pine Bluff added another field goal.

24–7.

The air felt heavy now.

Then something shifted.

Late in the third quarter, Tyler pulled on a counter and flattened a linebacker who never saw it coming. Cole cut off his hip and turned four yards into twelve.

The sideline noticed.

Early in the fourth quarter, Iron Valley scored. Methodical. No drama.

24–14.

The defense forced a three-and-out. Tyler clapped once as he jogged off the field. No celebration. Just business.

The headset crackled again.

The first two plays gained 8 yards, now a critical third and two.

"We've got the look," an assistant said. "If we check to it now, it's there."

Jack stared at the field.

The call made sense. Clean. Safe. Built for this moment. Something he could diagram and defend on film the next morning. We are getting four yards a carry. He could hear Ray's voice in his head, saying not to overthink it.

The assistant hovered beside him. Didn't push. Didn't argue. Just waited.

Jack glanced toward the huddle.

Helmets tilted toward the sideline. Hands on hips. Chests rising and falling. They were tired, but still together.

Tyler Briggs broke from the group and jogged halfway to the numbers. He didn't argue. Didn't sell it. Just met Jack's eyes.

"What do you see?" Jack asked.

"The safety is sitting on it. Let Cole rip it," Tyler said.

Jack nodded.

Tyler hesitated. "This week's theme."

It landed.

TRUST.

Cole stood just behind him now. He didn't speak at first, just gave the slightest eye roll. *You know this isn't it. Will you ever trust me?*

"We've repped it," Cole said. "They won't see it coming."

Jack looked back at the staff. The safe call still waited. Still clean. Still explainable.

Fear crept in.

Don't get cute.
Don't lose it trying to be right.

Sunday afternoons flashed through his mind—whiteboards full of answers that hadn't been enough. Asking kids to trust, then bailing when it mattered.

He looked back at Tyler. Then at Cole.

"You good?" Jack asked.

"Yes, sir," Tyler said.

Cole nodded once.

Jack exhaled. "Alright. Call it."

The ball was snapped.

For half a second, it looked wrong.

The back hesitated. The defense surged. A linebacker stepped downhill like he'd seen it coming.

Marcus came out of nowhere.

Hands high. Eyes steady. The ball dropped into his chest in stride.

Just space.

The stadium went quiet before it understood.

Marcus turned upfield.

Twenty-yard line.
Ten-yard line.

The last defender dove and missed.

Touchdown.

There was a beat of disbelief, players frozen, officials catching up, then the noise came. Helmets flew. The sideline erupted. Tyler slapped Cole's helmet hard enough to knock it sideways.

Jack didn't move.

He watched Marcus hand the ball to the official and jog back, calm, like this had always been the plan.

The assistant beside him let out a breath he'd been holding.

Jack nodded once, small, almost to himself.

It hadn't been safe.

It had been right.

24–21.

The crowd found its voice again.

Pine Bluff felt it.

They pressed. Forced a throw.

Interception.

Neil Parker sprinted to congratulate them.

Tyler helped Cole up after the return and said something Jack couldn't hear.

Cole nodded.

Two plays later, Tyler buried his man again. The run creased clean. Cole bounced it outside.

Touchdown.

Iron Valley took the lead at 28–24.

They had scored twenty-one points in the fourth quarter.

The final defensive stand felt like it lasted an hour.

Fourth down. Incomplete.

Ballgame.

Helmets flew. Players screamed. Parents hugged. The noise was different than the week before, less relief, more belief.

Jack found Megan and hugged her and Bennett quickly, before turning back to his team.

Jack found Tyler near the sideline, helmet off, chest heaving.

"You were right," Jack said.

Tyler shrugged. "We just kept pushing."

Jack watched him jog back toward his teammates, disappearing into the chaos like he always did.

Jack stood in the middle of the noise for a moment, watching the room. Most of the players were still celebrating, replaying the comeback in loud bursts.

One locker stayed quiet.

As the locker room slowly emptied, Jack noticed Neil still sitting at his locker, pads half-off, staring at the floor.

"You good?" Jack asked.

Neil looked up. "Yes, sir."

He hesitated.

"I just… I like being part of this. Thank you for letting me."

Jack nodded. He didn't say anything else.

As Jack turned off the lights and locked the door, he made a note to see what was going on with Neil.

Some leaders carried teams on their shoulders.
Others carried moments quietly, waiting for their turn.

And Neil Parker's story wasn't ready yet.

CHAPTER TWELVE

Neil

Last Season

Neil Parker liked being early.

Not because anyone told him to.
Not because he thought anyone would notice.

He just liked seeing things before they got loud.

The field looked different before practice. The lines were sharper. The air cooler. Helmets sat in rows, and the weight room doors were still closed. Even the wind sounded quieter, brushing across the bleachers in long, steady breaths.

Everything felt calm. Predictable.

Neil jogged a slow lap, then another, loosening his shoulders. A couple of linemen walked in through the gate, still half-asleep, but they didn't speak much yet. Morning belonged to the quiet people.

As Neil warmed up, he watched the field the way some people watched television. Not just looking—seeing.

A guard's stance—weight drifting onto his toes, heels barely touching the turf, the kind of balance that disappeared the moment someone attacked the edge.

A receiver's split—wide, but shoulders turned just enough to hint at a slant before the snap even came.

How far a safety drifted before the snap—three quiet steps toward the boundary, leaving a seam most people wouldn't notice unless they were looking for it.

Which players watched the quarterback… and which ones watched the backfield, eyes already dropping to the mesh point.

Little things.

Most people didn't notice little things.

Neil did.

He did the same thing every morning that season. Watching and observing in a way that was well beyond his years.

• • •

This Season

At home, mornings were steady.

His mom was already at the stove when he came into the kitchen, flipping eggs while toast browned in the toaster. The radio played softly, the same station it always did in the mornings.

"Morning," she said.

"Morning."

His dad sat at the table reading something on his phone, coffee in front of him, boots already on like he was halfway out the door even when he wasn't. He tapped the side of the mug twice with his thumb before every sip, the same way he always did when he was thinking.

Neil sat down and started eating.

"You got pads today?" his dad asked.

"Yeah."

His dad nodded once. "Good."

They ate quietly for a minute, the way families do when silence isn't uncomfortable. Forks on plates. The soft hiss of the stove. The announcer on the radio talking about the weather like it mattered more than it did.

"You ever think about coaching?" his dad asked suddenly.

Neil looked up. "Coaching?"

"Yeah."

Neil shrugged. "I'm not good enough at football to coach."

His dad smiled a little, not amused, just patient.

"Ability isn't something you control," he said. "Work ethic is. Paying attention is. The way you treat people is."

"You see things others don't see," he continued. "That is a gift that you can use to help others."

Neil didn't answer right away.

He thought about the depth chart posted in the locker room, his name still low, no promises.

He thought about scout-team bruises. Reps that didn't count on Fridays.

"I'm not sure anyone cares what I see," he said finally.

His dad looked at him steadily.

"They will," he said. "When it matters."

Neil looked back down at his plate.

They finished breakfast, grabbed their things, and headed out.

As Neil stepped out of the truck at the field house, his dad said one more thing.

"Keep working. I see you out there."

Then he reached over and squeezed Neil's shoulder once before leaning back again.

Neil nodded and shut the door.

The words stayed with him through the morning, simple, steady.

His dad didn't talk much.
But when he did, it mattered.

• • •

Present

Practice was loud by the time drills started.

Whistles. Music pumping from the sideline. Coaches shouting. Helmets popping. The rhythm of practice settled in the way it always did, chaotic on the surface, structured underneath.

Neil wasn't a starter. Everybody knew that, including him. He ran scout team most days. Special teams. Extra reps when someone needed one.

He didn't mind.

Football was still football.

During team period, Cole jogged over between reps and crouched beside him.

"What'd you see?" Cole asked quietly.

Neil looked at the defense.

"Safety's jumping Marcus," he said. "He's leaning that way before the snap. Not much—but he's cheating it."

Cole nodded once and jogged back into the huddle.

The next play, Cole opened to Marcus' side, held the safety with his eyes just long enough, then came back and threw backside.

Touchdown.

A couple of receivers slapped Cole's helmet. Coaches reset the ball. Practice rolled on like nothing had happened.

Neil didn't react. Just watched the play finish, then turned back toward the sideline.

A few minutes later, Tyler walked past and tapped his helmet.

"Good eye," Tyler said.

Neil nodded.

Moments like that mattered more than people realized.

Not because he needed praise.

Because it meant he was part of it.

• • •

After practice, most of the team headed in.

Neil stayed behind for a few minutes, helping carry a tackling dummy and stack cones near the shed. Nobody asked him to. He just did it.

The field was quiet again by the time he finished.

He sat on the bench, helmet beside him, watching the sun sink behind the bleachers. The light stretched long across the turf, turning the yard lines gold.

The stadium looked different in the evening light. Slower. Like it was catching its breath.

Neil thought about what his dad had said that morning.

Ability isn't something you control.
Work ethic is.

He wasn't the fastest.
Wasn't the strongest.
Probably never would be.

But he understood the game.

And he loved it.

That counted for something.

• • •

That night, Neil and his dad sat on the couch watching a college game.

They didn't talk much, just watched. The room was dim except for the glow of the television. Somewhere down the hall, his mom was folding laundry, the quiet rhythm of hangers clicking together drifting in and out.

Midway through the second quarter, Neil leaned forward slightly.

"That linebacker," he said. "He's reading his key late."

His dad watched the next play.

The offense ran right past the linebacker's gap.

His dad smiled. "You see it."

Neil shrugged, but he felt something settle inside him.

Not pride.

Something steadier than that.

Confidence.

Not in being the best.

In knowing he understood something that mattered.

But part of him still wondered if it would ever translate to more than scout-team reps. And if understanding the game was enough when the depth chart said otherwise.

He didn't say that part out loud.

• • •

At practice the next day, Cole jogged over again between periods.

"What'd you see?" he asked.

Neil answered, the same as always, calm, precise.

And for the first time, he realized something without needing anyone to say it:

He might never be the player everyone watched.

But he was the player other players trusted to see what they couldn't.

CHAPTER THIRTEEN

Finish What You Start

Whatever Iron Valley felt building the week before didn't carry across the field.

River Bend had won the last six meetings, and they lined up with the calm confidence of a team that expected a seventh.

They hit as if none of it mattered.
Because to them, it didn't.

Older. Disciplined. Built the way programs were supposed to be built. They didn't beat themselves. They didn't blink. They waited for you to make mistakes and then punished you without apology.

Jack liked teams like that.

They told the truth about your team.

Monday's film session was different. Not tense. Not loud. Just honest.

"They're better than the teams we've played," Jack said, pausing the screen. "Stronger up front. Faster in space. They won't wait on us to mess up."

The room stayed quiet.

"That's not a problem," Jack continued. "That's a test."

Tyler Briggs leaned forward in his chair.
Jack noticed.

The word of the week went up before practice.

FINISH

A couple of players glanced at it.

"Finish what?" someone asked.

Jack capped the marker.

"Everything."

No speech.
No explanation.

They understood.

• • •

Finish showed up in the details.

A lineman staying on a block just long enough.
A back driving his feet instead of stepping out early.
A receiver running through the whistle, even when he wasn't the first read.

Tyler stayed late every day that week.

He walked younger linemen through footwork after the whistle. Stood behind them during indy, correcting hand placement with a tap instead of a shout. Re-ran reps he didn't need just so they wouldn't be alone in it.

Between drills, he pulled a freshman aside and showed him where the game sped up, and where it didn't.

• • •

After most of the players had already gone in, the field lights hummed overhead and the last of the equipment was being carried toward the shed.

Tyler stood near the numbers, helmet hanging from one hand, staring out at the field.

Jack walked over. "Good work today."

Tyler nodded, but didn't move.

They stood there a few seconds in the quiet.

Then Tyler said, "I don't get it."

Jack waited.

"Why would he leave?" Tyler asked. "We're finally getting somewhere."

Jack looked out across the field but didn't answer.

Tyler looked at him then, not angry, just waiting, like he expected an answer that never came.

After a moment, Tyler said quietly, "I know it was about Marcus. Everybody knows."

The lights buzzed overhead. A door shut somewhere inside the field house.

Tyler looked back out at the field.

"I hate he isn't here right now," he said.

Jack nodded once. "I do too."

They stood there another moment before Jack said quietly, "I know this much. He cared about you. About all of you. That didn't change."

Tyler shook his head slightly.

"It's easy to say things," he said. "Harder to actually stick around."

The words hung in the air. Not disrespectful, just honest.

Jack let them sit there a second.

"Yeah," he said quietly. "It is."

Neither of them spoke for a few seconds, the lights buzzing softly above them, the field empty and still.

Finally, Tyler shifted his helmet under his arm and started toward the locker room.

Jack stayed where he was a few seconds longer, looking out across the field, the regret settling heavier than he expected.

He wished it hadn't gone the way it had. Wished there had been another conversation, another way to hold the staff together without backing away from what they were trying to build. But there hadn't been.

And building something, he was learning, sometimes meant losing people you respected along the way.

He turned off the lights and walked in.

• • •

Marcus and Cole found each other the same way they always had, without forcing it.

Cole talked. Marcus listened. Marcus worked. Cole noticed.

They pushed each other through drills. Celebrated small things. Helmet taps. Quiet nods.

During inside run one afternoon, Marcus came out of a rep shaking his head, frustrated at a missed read. Cole caught him before the next snap, said two quick words, and pointed at the linebacker's first step. Marcus nodded once, lined back up, and hit the next rep clean.

Nothing dramatic.
Just work.

Neil drifted into that orbit naturally.

At first, he stood a step outside the circle, listening more than talking. But on the scout team that week, something started to show.

Neil began making plays.

Not because he was faster or stronger, but despite this, he kept ending up in the right place. Slipping into throwing lanes. Breaking on routes a step early. Seeing things that other players didn't notice yet.

After one team period, he caught Cole walking back toward the huddle.

"Hey," Neil said quietly.

Cole turned.

Neil hesitated a second, like he wasn't sure if he should say anything.

"I can tell where you're going sometimes," he said.

Cole raised an eyebrow. "How?"

Neil pointed lightly toward his own face. "Your eyes. Before the snap."

Cole looked at him, not defensive, just curious now.

"You look at it a split second early," Neil said. "Not long. But it's there."

Cole didn't answer right away.

The next rep, he lined up and kept his eyes straight ahead longer than usual.

Marcus caught the ball on a dig behind the linebacker.

As they jogged back, Cole tapped Neil lightly on the shoulder pads as he passed.

Nothing said. But noticed.

From then on, Neil wasn't standing outside the circle anymore.

He was part of it.

He wasn't a contributor on Friday nights yet. But he belonged.

By Wednesday, something was obvious.

Iron Valley wasn't trying to prove anything anymore.

No speeches after drills.
No looking toward the sideline for approval.
Just helmets down, reps finished, players jogging back to the huddle already thinking about the next snap.

They weren't chasing belief anymore.

They were just working.

• • •

Friday night felt heavy.

River Bend scored first. Long drive. No panic. No celebration.

Iron Valley answered. Shorter drive. Efficient.

The game stayed tight. Every yard mattered. Every hit carried weight.

Late in the third quarter, River Bend drove inside the twenty.

Slow. Methodical. The kind of drive that used to break Iron Valley.

Third down. Power left.

Tyler met the puller in the hole. Marcus filled behind him and stopped the back a yard short.

Fourth down.

Field goal.

Jack exhaled slowly.

Last year, that drive ended in the end zone.

• • •

Early in the fourth quarter, Iron Valley faced fourth and two near midfield.

Cole jogged into the huddle, breathing hard but steady.

The call was simple.

The snap came. The line surged. The pile moved inches at a time. Slow, stubborn, finished.

First down.

Nothing spectacular. Just finished.

Late in the fourth quarter, Iron Valley trailed by four.

Timeout.

Jack looked at the offense gathered in front of him.

"We've been here before," he said. "Finish the game."

Tyler nodded. Marcus met Jack's eyes. Cole didn't say anything.

The call wasn't special.

Execution was.

Cole scrambled right, bought time, and Marcus saw it at the same moment. He broke his route late, slipped behind coverage, and caught the ball in stride.

Touchdown.

Iron Valley held on.

• • •

When the horn sounded, it didn't feel like relief.

It felt earned.

Then the realization hit.

Three and one.
One and zero in conference.

For the first time in twenty years.

The locker room erupted, helmets banging lockers, players shouting the record to hear it again, laughter spilling into the hallway.

Tyler sat down for a moment, breathing hard, smiling in a way Jack hadn't seen before. Marcus leaned against the wall, shaking his head, still trying to process it.

Jack let them have it.

They'd earned that noise. When it settled, he spoke briefly.

"Anybody can start fast," he said quietly.
"Good teams finish."

Heads nodded.

They understood.

• • •

Saturday morning found Jack standing along the fence at Bennett's youth game.

Bennett lined up at linebacker.

Across from him stood Dylan.

Marcus's little brother.

They collided on a sweep, both popping up laughing, shoving each other as they ran back to the huddle.

Kids didn't carry things yet.
Not the way older players did.

• • •

That afternoon, Marcus came by the house.

Dylan came with him.

Megan noticed the shoes first.

Too small. Worn thin.

Then the clothes. A hoodie that had clearly belonged to someone bigger once, the sleeves pushed back to keep his hands free.

Dylan ate quietly but quickly, trying not to look hungry.

Neil sat nearby laughing with Cole, relaxed, at ease in a way that came from not worrying about meals or rides or what waited at home.

Megan didn't say anything.

She just cooked more.

Refilled plates without asking.
Set a second helping down before anyone had to look up.

Dylan thanked her every time, polite in the way kids get when they've learned not to expect much.

When the boys started drifting outside, Megan stayed in the kitchen a few minutes longer.

Jack watched her open the cabinet, then the refrigerator, then pull out a couple of containers.

She packed them without saying anything—pasta, bread, a few pieces of chicken wrapped in foil, a bag of fruit from the counter.

Marcus came back in to grab a drink and stopped when he saw what she was doing.

"That's for later," Megan said, like it was the most ordinary thing in the world.

Marcus hesitated just a second, then nodded.

"Thank you, ma'am," he said quietly.

Dylan stood beside him, setting his container down so he could go outside.

Later, as the boys spilled into the yard again, Megan leaned beside Jack at the counter.

"They're hungry," she said softly.

Jack nodded.
"In more ways than one."

He watched Marcus in the backyard, showing Dylan how to throw a tighter spiral, patient, steady, never raising his voice.

Some kids were learning football.

Some kids were learning how to carry more than they should.

• • •

By Sunday morning, the noise had shifted.

The school's football page posted the final score.

The comments came quickly.

Congrats on beating cupcakes.
Try playing real teams.
Barely won.

Jack didn't scroll long.

The kids did.

Cole found Jack after his coaches' meeting, leaning in the doorway while assistants packed up.

"They're running their mouths," Cole said.

Jack nodded. "That's what they do."

"They don't think we're real."

Jack met his eyes. "Good."

Cole smiled slightly. "Marcus says let 'em think that."

Jack watched him head back down the hallway, the sounds of the locker room echoing behind him.

Winning a few games was one thing.

Learning to stay steady when the work got harder and the attention got louder, that was something else.

And five miles up the road, West Ridge was starting to notice.

CHAPTER FOURTEEN

Pressure Doesn't Ask Permission

Jack knew the athletic director wasn't asking him to stop by just to talk football.

"Come on in," the AD said, motioning toward the chair across from his desk.

Jack sat.

"Good win Friday," the AD said.

"Thank you. Hope this meeting goes better than the last one." Jack half-joked.

The AD leaned back in his chair and laughed. "Much better. People are excited."

Jack nodded but didn't answer.

"They should be," the AD said. "It's been a long time since this town had something to believe in."

He slid a paper across the desk.

"We adjusted your contract. Nothing huge. Just something to show we believe in what you're building."

Jack glanced at the number. It wasn't life-changing. But it wasn't nothing either.

"I appreciate it," Jack said.

The AD studied him a moment. "Just remember, when people start believing, expectations follow."

Jack nodded. "I know."

Walking back down the hallway, Jack realized the raise wasn't what stayed with him.

It was the weight behind it.

Pressure didn't arrive loudly. It settled in quietly.

It smiled first. It shook hands. It said things like proud and finally and we believe in you now.

And then it got heavy.

Parents lingered longer after practice now. Phones came out faster. People who hadn't said much all year suddenly had opinions about what Iron Valley could be.

Pressure didn't shout.

It watched.

• • •

Monday afternoon, the locker room was quieter than usual.

Not tired.
Not distracted.

Just listening.

Jack waited until everyone was seated before he walked to the whiteboard. He didn't say anything at first. Just uncapped the marker and wrote one word in block letters.

POISE

He stepped back and let them look at it.

No one spoke.

After a moment, Jack turned around.

"Pressure shows up in a lot of ways," he said. "Sometimes it's a scoreboard. Sometimes it's a crowd. Sometimes it's a phone in your hand."

A few players shifted in their seats. Cole kept his eyes on the board.

"Most people think pressure makes you stronger," Jack continued. "It doesn't. Pressure just shows what's already there."

He let that sit a second.

"Poise," he said, tapping the board lightly, "is the ability to stay the same when everything around you wants to speed you up."

No speeches. No pacing. Just quiet words in a still room.

"You don't need to play harder," Jack said. "You need to keep your focus when it would be easy to lose your poise."

Tyler sat forward, elbows on his knees, listening the way he always did when something mattered.

Jack glanced around the room.

"Crowds get louder. Expectations get higher. People start watching you different. That's normal. That's what happens when you start doing something right."

He paused.

"But poise means you don't change just because the noise does."

The room was still.

Neil looked down at his hands, turning the tape on his fingers slowly. Marcus leaned back, eyes on the word, expression unreadable. Cole sat quietly, shoulders relaxed now, breathing slower than he had been all morning.

Jack capped the marker.

"That's it," he said. "Let's go to work."

Chairs slid back. Helmets came up. The room moved again, but slower than usual, like everyone was carrying something they didn't want to drop.

On the board, the word stayed.

POISE.

• • •

Practice felt sharper.

Tyler Briggs was already sweating before the team period started. He finished every drill like the rep mattered more than the last one. Running to the next station. Finishing blocks ten yards downfield. Saying very little.

Pressure showed up differently in seniors.

Some talked more.
Some carried it in silence.

Tyler worked.

He stayed even longer after practices with a growing group of young offensive linemen who looked to him as the leader.

• • •

Before practice the next day, Cole waited near the lockers.

"Dad," he said quietly.

Jack looked up.

Cole held out his phone.

"You see this?"

Jack glanced down.

A graphic from the next opponent. Cole's picture. A score prediction underneath. Comments stacking up.

Most of it was predictable.

Trash talk. Predictions. Laughing emojis.

Then he saw one that wasn't trying to be funny.

How to win in spite of your QB.

Jack scrolled once.

Underneath it were likes.

A few from the other team. And a few from names Jack recognized.

Kids from Iron Valley.

Jack handed the phone back without reacting.

Cole watched his face, trying to read it.

"You alright?" Jack asked.

Cole lied and nodded. "Yeah."

Jack studied him for a second. Shoulders tight. Jaw set.

"Good," Jack said quietly. "Then it's already losing."

Cole slid the phone into his locker.

A minute later, helmets went on, and practice started.

Jack noticed the first few reps of team period, Cole's feet just a little fast, reads just a little rushed.

Pressure showed up in small ways first.

• • •

Marcus was quieter in meetings that week.

Not distracted.
Just somewhere deeper in his own head.

He stayed after practice that evening.

Not alone—there were always a few players finishing lifts or taping ankles—but longer than most. Running routes on air, catching balls from the machine Evans had left plugged in near the sideline.

Same route.
Same break.
Same catch.

Jack watched from the office window for a minute before stepping outside.

Marcus saw him but didn't stop.

"You good?" Jack asked.

Marcus nodded, breathing hard. "Yes, sir."

Jack waited.

Marcus looked down at the turf.

"My aunt called today," he said finally. "Mom's back in the hospital."

Jack didn't answer right away.

Marcus kept talking, like the silence had given him permission.

"They say it's nothing serious," he said. "But that's what they always say."

Jack nodded once.

Marcus swallowed. "I just don't want to be somewhere else when something happens."

Jack let that sit.

"You're here," he said finally. "So be here."

Marcus nodded slowly. "Yes, sir."

Jack put a hand briefly on his shoulder and walked back toward the building.

Marcus turned back and ran the route again.

This time he caught the ball clean and didn't drop it when he hit the ground.

Jack noticed.

Pressure didn't always break people.

Sometimes it just made them quieter.

• • •

That afternoon, Tyler stayed late again, working footwork in silence. Cones were still lined up from indy period, and he moved through them slowly, resetting his hands each step like he was teaching his body not to forget.

Marcus stayed too, running routes in the fading light, saying nothing.

Cole threw for another twenty minutes after everyone else had left, working timing routes with a freshman receiver who looked surprised just to be there.

Jack watched from the doorway for a moment before heading in.

Pressure didn't hit everyone the same way. But it hit everyone.

• • •

Another Friday night filled with pressure.

Mountain View came in with a winning record. Disciplined. Patient. Experienced group that was well coached and would challenge Iron Valley.

Jack liked teams like that.

They exposed the truth.

Mountain View scored first. A long drive. Nothing flashy. Just clean execution and no mistakes.

Iron Valley answered later, grinding out a drive that took patience. Tyler sealed the edge on a third-down run that kept it alive. Marcus caught one ball in traffic and held on. Cole managed the rest.

The game stayed tight.

Every series felt like it mattered a little more than it should.

But something was off with Cole.

Jack saw it on the second drive. RPO to the field side, the defensive end crashed hard inside, and the pull read was as clean as it gets. Wide open edge. Six yards minimum. Cole handed the ball off into a stacked box for a gain of one.

Jack marked it mentally and moved on.

Third drive. Same concept. Same look. The end squeezed down, the overhang player bit on the run fake, and the alley opened up like a hallway. Cole gave the ball away again. The back got swallowed at the line.

Jack felt his jaw tighten.

He told himself it was the game. Mountain View was physical. Maybe Cole was seeing something he wasn't. Maybe the angles looked different from behind center.

But he knew better.

Midway through the third quarter, the game was knotted at ten. Iron Valley faced third and four near midfield. Jack sent in the RPO again, the same concept they had repped a hundred times that week. Tyler would seal the edge. Marcus would clear out the corner. If the end crashed, Cole pulls it and walks into the first down.

The end crashed.

Cole handed it off.

The back hit a wall of bodies at the line and went nowhere. Fourth down. Punt.

Jack was already moving before the whistle died.

Cole jogged toward the bench, pulling his chinstrap loose. He didn't look at the sideline. He knew what was coming.

Jack met him at the numbers.

"What are you doing out there?" Jack's voice was louder than he meant it to be, but he didn't pull it back. "That's your ball. Three times tonight the end has crashed and three times you've given it away. You have the easiest read on the field and you won't take it."

Cole's jaw set. He stared straight ahead, past Jack, at the scoreboard.

"I'm reading it, Coach."

"You're not reading anything. You're hiding from the ball." Jack stepped closer, pointing back at the field. "We didn't build this offense so you could hand it off every snap and hope somebody else makes a play. If you've got the pull, you pull it. That's not optional."

Marcus stood a few feet away, helmet in his hands, watching the turf like it might open up and swallow him. Tyler had turned his back, pretending to adjust his gloves, but his shoulders were tight and still. Neil stood at the edge of the group, quiet and motionless, eyes moving between Cole and Jack like he was watching something break in real time.

Across the sideline, Coach Evans stood with his arms folded, watching Jack, not Cole.

Cole finally looked at his father. Not apologetic. Not soft. Something harder than that, the look a kid gets when the thing eating at him is bigger than anything he's being yelled at for, and he knows saying it out loud won't fix it.

"I'm doing the best I can."

His voice was flat. Controlled. But it cracked at the edges in a way that had nothing to do with football.

Then he walked to the far end of the bench and sat down alone.

Jack stood there for a second, heart still pounding from the exchange, and turned back toward the field. The defense was already lining up.

He put his headset back on.

The game kept going.

Nobody on the sideline said a word about what they'd just seen. But the air had changed, the way it does when something private becomes public and everyone pretends it didn't.

Late in the fourth quarter, the scoreboard felt louder than the crowd.

Iron Valley led by seven.

But it didn't feel safe.

The chains moved after Cole dove forward on fourth down, the ball pinned tight against his chest as bodies collapsed around him. The official's arm shot forward.

First down.

The sideline exhaled, but only halfway.

The clock kept moving.

Jack stepped closer to the numbers, headset hanging loose around his neck. He didn't yell. Didn't signal wildly. The moment didn't need noise.

It needed control.

Players gathered near him between snaps, helmets tilted toward the field, eyes drifting to the clock more than the defense.

"We're fine," Jack said calmly. "This is what poise looks like."

Tyler nodded once, hands on his hips, breathing heavy but steady. Marcus stared across the line, already studying leverage. Cole stayed quiet, eyes locked on the defense tightening its front, pressure creeping closer with every second draining away.

Every play felt shorter. Every huddle quicker. The stadium buzz sharpened, restless, waiting for something to break.

Iron Valley lined up again.

No hurry. No panic.

Just execution.

Neil stood a few steps behind him, helmet in hand, watching the front the way he always did, not the ball, not the crowd, just the defense.

Cole glanced at him. "What do you see?"

Neil didn't hesitate.

"The end's crashing every time," he said quietly. "Nobody's outside if you pull it."

Cole looked back at the line again, seeing it now the same way. The edge felt wider. Slower. Predictable.

The other sideline sensed the moment tightening too.

Cole stepped under center, eyes scanning the front Neil had pointed out.

Clap.

Snap.

Cole rode the mesh a beat longer, then pulled the ball cleanly and slid outside. No explosion. No hero run. Just enough space to move the chains and force the defense to chase instead of attack.

Jack folded his arms on the sideline.

Poise wasn't about doing more.

It was about seeing clearly when everything around you wanted you to rush.

The clock bled under a minute.

Across the field, defenders barked louder now, urgency replacing confidence. Iron Valley didn't answer with emotion. They answered by lining up again.

Cole looked toward the sideline once.

Jack met his eyes and simply nodded.

No words.

They didn't need them anymore.

The ball was snapped again, and the seconds kept disappearing, slow enough to feel every one of them.

Iron Valley wasn't trying to win the moment.

They were managing it.

And for the first time all night, the pressure belonged to someone else.

When the horn sounded, it didn't feel like relief.

It felt earned.

Four in a row.

• • •

The celebration afterward was shorter.

Parents drifted down from the stands. A few pictures. Handshakes. Smiles.

Jack stood near the numbers, watching.

He saw Cole near the fence talking with Megan. She was smiling, saying something Jack couldn't hear. Cole laughed—really laughed—for the first time all night.

Bennett stood between them, bouncing on his toes, talking fast about something only he seemed to understand.

Jack stayed where he was and let the moment belong to them.

Not the quarterback.

Just a family.

That was enough.

• • •

Later that night, the house was quieter than the week before.

Cole sat at the kitchen table, scrolling slowly on his phone.

The same post was still there.

More likes now.

Megan set a glass of water in front of him. "You need to get off that thing."

Cole slid the phone face down. "I know."

Bennett sat on the floor nearby, building a crooked stadium out of legos.

"You throw a touchdown?"

"Not tonight."

"That's okay," Bennett said. "You will next time."

Cole smiled a little.

Bennett looked up. "Why does everyone yell so much at games?"

Cole laughed quietly. "That's just what people do."

"They don't yell at my games," Bennett said. "They just clap."

Megan smiled faintly.

Bennett went back to lining up tiny plastic players across his crooked field, completely at peace in a world where games were simple and tomorrow always worked out.

Cole leaned back in his chair, watching him.

For a moment, the noise from the week felt far away.

Bennett didn't know about any of it.

He just believed things would work out.

Cole wasn't sure when people stopped believing that.

• • •

Cole went to bed first. Then Bennett, still talking about his lego stadium as Megan walked him down the hall.

The house got quiet.

Jack sat at the kitchen table, replaying the third-quarter RPO in his head for the fourth time. The end crashed. The pull was there. Cole gave it away. Three times.

He was right about the read. He was sure about that.

The back door opened.

Evans stood in the doorway, jacket still on, keys in his hand. He had that look, the one assistants get when they know something the head coach doesn't and they're not sure how it's going to land.

"Got a minute?" Evans asked.

Jack nodded toward the chair across from him.

Evans sat and set his phone on the table, screen facing Jack.

"It's not just the one post," Evans said. "It's been going on for a few weeks."

Jack looked at the screen. A parents' Facebook group. Iron Valley Football Families. Posts he'd never seen because no one had thought to show him, or maybe no one had wanted to.

The comments scrolled past in a blur, but certain lines stopped him cold.

Must be nice when daddy calls the plays.

How many carries does his kid need before he's satisfied?

Other kids work just as hard and don't get half the opportunities.

Coach's son shouldn't be getting the ball every play. It's obvious.

Jack scrolled further. Some names he didn't recognize. Some he did. Parents who shook his hand after games. Parents whose kids he'd coached up, stayed late for, driven home after practice.

"That one's from last Tuesday," Evans said, pointing. "The day after the River Bend game."

Jack stared at it.

Funny how the QB keeps getting carries when we've got other backs sitting on the bench. Guess bloodlines matter more than talent at Iron Valley.

Evans let the silence hold for a few seconds.

"He's seen all of it," Evans said. "I don't know how long, but he's seen it. Couple of the kids have been showing him stuff too, thinking they're being funny, not realizing what it's doing."

Jack set the phone down.

"Why didn't you tell me sooner?" he asked.

Evans met his eyes. "I didn't know how deep it was until tonight. After what happened on the sideline, I started asking around."

Jack leaned back in his chair and stared at the ceiling.

Evans stood up. "I'm not telling you what to do, Coach. I just thought you should know what he's been carrying."

He left through the back door. The latch clicked softly behind him.

Jack sat there for a long time.

He picked up Evans's words and turned them over in his head. What he's been carrying. He thought about Cole handing the ball off into stacked boxes. Giving away clean reads. Shrinking on the field. And then he thought about himself, standing at the numbers, yelling at his son for not pulling the ball, in front of Marcus, in front of Tyler, in front of Neil, in front of everyone.

Cole wasn't missing reads.

He was trying to disappear.

And Jack, the coach who built his whole philosophy around seeing kids for who they were, hadn't seen the one standing right in front of him.

He heard Megan's footsteps before he saw her.

She came into the kitchen in her robe, arms crossed, and leaned against the counter. She didn't sit down. That told him everything he needed to know about where this conversation was headed.

"You want to tell me what that was tonight?" she said.

Jack exhaled. "I was coaching him, Megan."

"You were embarrassing him."

The words landed harder than Jack expected.

"He had the pull three times and gave it away," Jack said. "That's my job to correct."

"Your job." She let the word sit there. "You screamed at your son in front of his teammates. In front of the whole sideline. In front of me."

Jack looked at the table.

"He doesn't get to go home to a different house after the game, Jack. He doesn't get to leave you at the stadium the way those other kids do. He sits at your table. He sleeps down the hall. And every time you coach him like that in front of everyone, he carries it into this house."

Jack opened his mouth.

"I'm not finished," Megan said.

He closed it.

"I don't care if the read was right. You can be right about the football and wrong about everything else at the same time." She paused. "And tonight, you were wrong about everything else."

Jack didn't argue. Not because he agreed completely, but because somewhere behind the defensiveness, he could feel the truth of it pressing against his chest.

"Those parents are saying things about him," Jack said quietly. "Evans just showed me. Our own parents."

Megan's expression didn't change. "I know."

Jack looked up.

"I've known for weeks," she said. "Because I pay attention to what's happening in this family, not just what's happening on that field."

That one cut deeper than any of it.

She stood there another moment, then unfolded her arms.

"Fix it," she said. "Not the football part. The father part."

She walked back down the hall.

Jack sat alone at the kitchen table for a long time. The house was dark except for the light over the stove. He could hear the refrigerator hum and nothing else.

He thought about Evan from last year. The kid whose face told him everything he needed to know, and he'd raised a hand and stopped him from saying it.

He thought about standing on the sideline tonight, pointing at the field, telling his son he was hiding from the ball.

He thought about Cole walking to the far end of the bench and sitting down alone.

Different kid. Same mistake.

Jack was still sitting there when the stove light flickered once and steadied.

He didn't have the words yet.

But he knew he'd have to find them.

Sunday morning brought the noise back.

By the time film started, several coaches had already seen the posts.

More comments.
More predictions.
More people talking.

Jack let them settle into their seats before walking to the board.

He wrote one word.

RESPONSE

He didn't circle it.
Didn't explain it.
Just left it there.

No one asked what it meant. They already knew.

• • •

That night, Jack stood alone on the field.

The stands were empty. The air was still.

Winning felt good.

But keeping it felt heavier.

And for the first time, Jack understood something he hadn't fully grasped before: pressure wasn't a sign that something was wrong.

It was a sign that something mattered.

He turned off the lights and walked toward the tunnel.

They would find out soon enough what pressure revealed.

CHAPTER FIFTEEN

Megan

Last Season

Megan didn't like being in the stands.

At their previous school, she rarely noticed the crowd. Winning had a way of softening everything—the noise, the criticism, even the long nights. People were patient when you won. Kind, even.

Iron Valley was different.

That first season, she learned quickly that losing changed how people sounded.

She remembered one of the early games, sitting halfway up the home bleachers as the fourth quarter drained away and the score slipped further out of reach. The crowd had thinned some, but the ones who stayed weren't always the ones you hoped would.

A group of men sat a few rows behind her.

They were talking and shouting most of the game.

"This guy sucks."
"I could call a better game than this."
"No wonder we can't finish. Coach is just standing there."

Megan sat still.

She didn't turn around. Didn't react. She just watched the field, hands folded in her lap, listening to strangers talk about the man she knew better than anyone.

They didn't see what she saw.

They didn't see him awake at two in the morning, staring at a notebook he wasn't writing in.

They didn't see the weight he carried home every Friday night.

They didn't see how little he slept.

By midseason, Jack had lost fifteen pounds. His face had grown sharper. His eyes looked tired even on mornings when he tried to act normal.

One night she woke up and found him sitting on the edge of the bed, elbows on his knees, staring at the floor.

"You okay?" she asked softly.

He shook his head.

"I don't know if I can fix this," he said quietly. "I don't know if I'm the right guy for this place."

It was the first time she had ever heard him say something like that.

Jack had always been steady. Not loud. Not emotional. Just certain.

That season, certainty had left him.

After every loss, they sat at the kitchen table long after Cole had gone to bed. Jack would replay moments, not play calls, not schemes, but decisions. Conversations. Things he wished he had said differently.

"I keep thinking I'm missing something," he told her once. "Something they need that I'm not giving them."

Megan listened.

She didn't try to fix it. She knew better than that.

"You're still showing up," she said.

Jack looked at her, tired.

"I don't know if that's enough."

"It is," she said quietly. "Maybe not today. But it is."

The next morning, he got up before the alarm, just like always.

He shaved. Put on his school shirt. Drank his coffee standing at the counter.

And went back to work.

He kept at it every day.

Even when the stands got ugly.
Even when the losses piled up.
Even when doubt sat heavy in the house like humidity you couldn't escape.

Megan had realized something that season, sitting in those stands, listening to people who only saw Friday nights.

They thought winning only showed up on a scoreboard.
They thought leadership meant yelling.
They thought belief was of no consequence.

They were wrong.

Belief looked like a man getting up on Monday morning when everything in him wanted to stay in bed, showing up for kids who weren't sure they believed yet, and staying in a place where leaving would have been easier to explain than staying and doing the slow work that nobody sees.

Megan watched Jack walk off the field that night, shoulders heavy but steps steady.

She knew something the crowd didn't.

He would get up tomorrow.

And the day after that.

And the day after that.

No matter how long it took.

• • •

Present

The house was quiet again.

Megan stood at the sink, rinsing plates one at a time, listening to the last of the voices fade outside as car doors shut and engines started. The team meal had ended the way it always did—slowly, boys lingering in the kitchen, on the couch, in the yard, nobody in a hurry to leave.

Now it was just the hum of the refrigerator and the soft clink of dishes.

She dried her hands and looked around the kitchen.

Empty cups on the counter. A chair pushed back crookedly. A hoodie draped over the back of a stool that someone would probably forget until Monday.

She folded it neatly and set it by the door.

Jack sat at the table, elbows resting on the wood, staring at nothing in particular. He wasn't tired in the way most people meant tired. It was deeper than that. The kind that settled behind the eyes.

"You going to bed?" Megan asked.

"In a minute," he said.

She nodded. She had learned a long time ago that "in a minute" didn't mean a minute. It meant he was still replaying things he wished he could do over.

She turned off the kitchen light over the sink and left the one above the table on.

Jack stayed there a while longer.

• • •

The next afternoon, Megan pulled into the school parking lot to pick up Bennett.

Kids were spilling out of the doors in groups, laughing, backpacks slung over their shoulders, talking about homework, practice, and weekend plans.

She stepped inside to wait near the office.

"Things must be exciting right now," one of the office secretaries said as she walked by. "Winning like this. The town hasn't talked about anything else all week."

Megan smiled politely.

"It's good for the kids," she said.

The woman nodded. "Still, must be fun."

Megan hesitated just a moment.

"It's not really about fun," she said gently. "It's about them."

The secretary looked a little surprised, then nodded again. "Well… you all are doing something right."

Megan thanked her and turned as Bennett came down the hallway, already talking before he reached her.

She listened, smiling, but her mind lingered on the conversation.

People saw Friday nights.
The lights.
The crowd.
The noise.

They didn't see the quiet parts.

• • •

That evening, Jack came home later than usual.

He set his keys on the counter and stood there a moment, like he wasn't quite ready to sit down yet. Megan watched him from the stove, noticing the way his shoulders sagged, the way he exhaled slowly before finally pulling out a chair.

She set a plate in front of him.

They ate quietly for a few minutes. Not uncomfortable silence, just the kind that settles in when someone is tired enough that words feel heavy.

Jack finally set his fork down.

"I watched Cole walk off the field today," he said. "He didn't look back. Not at me, not at anyone. Just walked straight to the locker room like he couldn't get away from me fast enough."

Megan pulled out the chair across from him and sat down.

"Do you know what I saw today?" she asked.

Jack looked up.

"I saw Cole helping a freshman with his stance after practice," she said. "Nobody asked him to. He just did it. And he sounded exactly like you."

Jack rubbed a hand across his face. "I keep telling myself I'm building something for these kids. But what if I'm building it on top of my own son?"

"He's not running from you, Jack," Megan said, her voice calm but firm. "He's becoming you. The good parts."

Jack didn't answer.

"You're so worried about what you're taking from him," she continued, "that you can't see what you're giving him."

Jack leaned back in his chair, staring at the table.

"I keep thinking about what Cole's going to remember," he said quietly. "Not the wins. Not the team. Whether his dad was the coach who built something or the one who wasn't there when it counted."

Megan nodded. She understood that. That part of him had always been there, the part that carried responsibility like it was something physical.

"You're not losing him," she said. "But you are doing one thing wrong."

Jack looked up, surprised.

"You're trying to carry all of it," she said. "And that's not your job."

Jack frowned slightly. "Then what is?"

"To lead them," she said. "Not to control every outcome. Not to fix every problem. Just to lead them."

The room was quiet for a moment.

Jack picked up his fork again, then set it back down without taking a bite.

"You really believe that?" he asked.

Megan met his eyes.

"I believe in you," she said. "But more than that, I believe in the work you're doing, whether anyone else sees it yet or not."

Jack sat there a long moment, letting that settle.

Outside, a car passed slowly down the street, headlights sliding across the kitchen wall and fading again.

Finally, Jack nodded.

Not because everything felt better.

But because he felt steadier.

And sometimes, Megan knew, that was enough.

• • •

Thursday nights were always the busiest.

Players came straight from practice, still smelling like grass and sweat, holding their cleats, voices loud in the way boys' voices always were when the work of the week was nearly done.

Shoes piled by the door. Plates balanced on knees. Laughter echoing down the hallway.

Megan was constantly taking care of all those at the table.

She watched Marcus eat quietly at the end of the table, focused in a way that wasn't about hunger alone. She saw Neil sitting nearby, listening more than talking, smiling at things others said.

Different kids. Different stories.

Same need.

At one point, she leaned against the counter and looked out into the living room.

Jack stood near the doorway, talking to a group of players, with one hand on a kid's shoulder, listening more than speaking.

She realized something then.

People thought the job happened under stadium lights.

Most of it happened in rooms like this.

In kitchens.
In conversations.
In moments nobody ever saw.

Later, when the house was quiet again, and the last car had gone, Megan walked through the living room picking up empty cups.

She paused for a moment, looking at the space.

The couch cushions were out of place. A blanket half-folded. The faint smell of food, grass and sweat still hung in the air.

It felt lived in.

Full.

She turned off the light and stood in the hallway for a moment. The house was still. She should have gone to bed.

Instead she sat back down at the kitchen table, pulled out her phone, and called Laura.

Laura picked up on the second ring, the way she always did, like no time had passed at all. They talked about nothing for a minute—Laura's daughter's soccer schedule, a neighbor who'd finally torn down that ugly fence. Normal things. Easy things.

Then Laura asked how she was doing. Really doing.

Megan opened her mouth to say the usual. Fine. Good. Busy.

But her voice caught.

"I'm good," she said. "The boys are good. Jack's good." She pressed her fingers against her eyes. "I just miss having someone to talk to."

She laughed a little, but it came out wrong—wet and thin, the kind that's holding back more than it lets through.

"The team moms are nice," she said, steadier now but not by much. "They're polite at games. They wave in the parking lot. But nobody's called just to check on me. Not once."

Laura said something soft on the other end. Something about visiting soon.

"I chose this," Megan said quietly. "I'd choose it again. I just didn't know it would feel this lonely."

Down the hall, Jack stood in the dark.

He'd gotten up for water. That was all. But when he heard her voice from the kitchen—low, uneven, nothing like the voice she used during the day—he stopped.

He didn't move. Didn't interrupt. Just stood there and listened to his wife say out loud the things she'd never say to him.

He heard her hang up. Heard her take a long breath. Heard her pull herself back together the way she always did—quiet and deliberate, like folding something heavy into a small space.

He waited a beat, then walked into the kitchen like he'd just come down the hall.

Megan was wiping the counter. Her eyes were a little red, but she smiled when she saw him. Bright. Normal.

"Thought you went to bed," she said.

"Just getting water."

She nodded and turned back to the counter.

Jack didn't get water. He crossed the kitchen and wrapped his arms around her from behind. Didn't say a word. Just held her.

Megan went still for a second. Then her hand came up and rested on his forearm, and she exhaled—a long, slow breath, like she'd been holding it for weeks.

They stood like that for a while. Neither of them spoke.

He didn't tell her what he'd heard. She didn't ask why he was really there. Some things didn't need words. They just needed someone to show up.

The team didn't just belong to the school.

Part of it lived here now.

And she was okay with that.

CHAPTER SIXTEEN

Some Losses Leave Bruises

Jack had been the new kid more times than he could count.

He'd learned early how to travel light, how not to attach too much to places that might not keep him.

Now, standing in the field house and watching his own players move through the room, he felt the irony settle.

These were kids he was asking to stay.

Stay when it hurt.
Stay when it wasn't fun.
Stay when leaving would be easier to explain.

He watched Tyler Briggs lace his cleats slowly, methodically, the way someone does when they know exactly where they're going and don't need to rush to get there.

Jack had spent most of his life being the one who left.

He hadn't spent much time thinking about what it meant to be the one someone stayed for.

The morning after practice, the weight room was quiet.

Not empty, just drained.

The smell of drying sweat lingered in the air, sharp and stale, like effort that hadn't been rewarded yet. Bars sat racked where they'd been left. A lone towel lay crumpled near the squat rack, forgotten.

Jack moved through the room slowly. His knees ached. His shoulders felt heavier than they should have. He noticed the same in the kids, their steps a half-beat slower, laughter delayed, conversations shorter.

This was the part of the season no one talked about.

Not the excitement.
Not the hope.

The hangover.

And Central Heights was coming.

Conference games didn't care about momentum.

Seven games to decide whether you were real or just passing through. They didn't care about themes or progress or how long it had been since Iron Valley mattered. Conference games showed you exactly where you stood—and how far you still had to go.

Iron Valley was now 4-1, but 2-0 in conference.

Central Heights came in 5–0 and 2-0 in conference.

Eight straight wins over Iron Valley.

Big. Fast. Disciplined. The kind of team that warmed up like it expected to be playing in December. Their kids didn't talk much. They didn't look around. They just worked.

Jack noticed how their linemen never wasted steps. How their linebackers filled gaps without hesitation. How their receivers blocked like it mattered, because they'd been taught it mattered.

This wasn't Cedar Grove.
This wasn't River Bend.

This was real.

The word of the week—**CONSISTENCY**—felt heavier under the lights.

Central Heights scored first. No surprise. Twelve plays. Seven minutes gone. Every snap felt like a message.

Iron Valley answered.

Cole carried early. Hard runs. Low pads. No dancing. Marcus caught two passes on the opening drive—tough catches, traffic catches. The crowd leaned forward, hopeful but careful.

Then the hits came.

The first one rattled Marcus, but didn't stop him.
The second one stayed with him.
The third one changed him.

Marcus got up slower each time. His routes lost sharpness. His eyes stopped scanning. He dropped a pass he hadn't dropped all season.

Jack saw it.

Pulled him aside.

"You okay?" Jack asked.

Marcus nodded too fast. "I'm good."

Jack sent him back in anyway.

Two plays later, Marcus took another shot—helmet to ribs. He stayed down longer this time.

When he came off, he didn't make eye contact.

After that, Marcus disappeared.

Not physically.

Mentally.

Routes shortened. Hands tighter. Trust gone.

Jack adjusted.

Cole carried.

And carried.

And carried some more.

By halftime, Cole already had twenty touches.

Central Heights led by seven.

The third quarter didn't bring relief.

Iron Valley fought. Scratched. Hung on longer than anyone expected. Every possession felt like it cost something.

Cole carried the ball again.

And again.

And again.

By the middle of the third quarter, the hits were starting to change. Not the clean ones early in the game—the kind that knocked you down but let you bounce back. These were the late hits in the pile. Helmets driving into ribs. Hands grabbing jerseys and twisting as whistles blew.

Cole got up slower once.

Then again.

On the sideline, Jack watched him jog back to the huddle, shoulders rising and falling heavier than before. Cole never looked toward the bench. Never signaled for a sub. Just bent at the waist, hands on his thighs for a moment, then turned back toward the line.

"Forty's coming," Coach Evans said quietly beside Jack.

Jack nodded.

Cole took the next handoff and lowered his shoulder into a linebacker who outweighed him by thirty pounds. The collision echoed across the field. Cole stumbled, caught himself, and drove for two more yards before going down.

When he stood, he flexed his fingers once, shaking feeling back into them, then jogged back to the huddle.

He didn't limp.

But he didn't run the same either.

Late in the third quarter, Marcus took a vicious hit over the middle.

The ball fell incomplete, but no one noticed at first. The sound of the collision carried across the field—helmet to shoulder, bodies folding hard into the turf.

Marcus stayed down a moment.

Not dramatic. Not waving for help. Just still long enough that the sideline noticed.

He got up slowly and jogged to the sideline, one arm tight against his ribs.

The trainer met him near the bench.

"Sit down a minute," he said.

Marcus lowered himself onto the bench and pulled off his helmet, breathing harder than he wanted anyone to see. The trainer pressed along his side, asking quiet questions, checking for pain.

"You good to go back?" the trainer asked after a minute.

Marcus nodded automatically.

The trainer glanced toward Coach Evans. "He's okay," he said quietly. "Just knocked the wind out."

Evans nodded.

Marcus didn't move.

The trainer looked back at him. "You good?"

Marcus stared at the ground.

"I don't feel like I can," he said quietly.

The words were almost lost in the noise of the game.

A moment later, Neil came over, helmet in his hands, sweat running down the side of his face. He sat beside Marcus without saying anything at first, just watching the field.

"What's going on?" Neil finally asked.

Marcus shook his head slowly. "I don't know… I just—" He exhaled. "I feel like I've got nothing left."

Neil didn't answer right away. He just sat there with him, both of them staring at the field while the game moved on without them.

A few yards away, Jack glanced toward the bench and caught part of the exchange—not the words, just the posture, the stillness, the look on Marcus's face.

Jack looked back to the field.

The game wasn't slowing down.

And neither were the hits.

Cole took another carry and was driven backward this time, bodies piling on top of him, defenders taking an extra second to roll off. When he stood, he reached briefly for his side, then dropped his hand before anyone noticed.

Forty carries came and went.

The fourth quarter bled time.

Iron Valley had the ball late. Down four. One drive to steal something no one expected.

The huddle formed slowly. Breathing heavy. Jerseys dark with sweat. Helmets tilted slightly lower than they had been in the first quarter.

Cole stepped in, hands on his hips, chest rising hard.

"Let's go," he said quietly.

No speeches. No shouting.

Just that.

They moved the ball in small pieces. Three yards. Four. A short pass. A scramble.

Every snap felt heavier than the last.

Then fourth down.

Cole took the snap.

Ran.

Central Heights stopped them a yard short.

The whistle blew.

For a moment, no one moved.

Turnover on downs.

Then the horn sounded.

Central Heights celebrated. Not wild. Just satisfied. Helmets raised. Hands slapped. A job finished.

Iron Valley stood still.

Jack felt it then, not anger, not frustration.

Hurt.

The kind that settled behind your ribs and stayed there.

• • •

The locker room was silent.

Jack didn't speak right away.

He didn't trust his voice.

Cole sat with his head back against the locker, chest heaving. Marcus stared at the floor, pads untouched.

Jack stood in front of them.

He didn't pace. He didn't raise his voice.

"Nobody's coming to save us," he said.

A few heads dropped.

"That's not bad news," Jack continued. "That's the point."

Silence.

"Every program in this league has reasons," he said. "Injuries. Youth. Bad calls. Tough schedules. You want excuses, they're everywhere. They're easy to find."

He paused.

"Losers live there."

No one moved.

"Some people don't just want excuses," Jack went on. "They want someone to make them feel better about why it didn't work. Why it wasn't their fault."

He shook his head once.

"That's not us."

Jack looked around the room, meeting eyes one at a time.

"We're going to be a program that finds a way. Not when it's fair. Not when it's clean. Not when it's convenient. But in all situations."

He let it sit.

"When it hurts. When it's heavy. When nobody feels sorry for us."

Cole lifted his head.

Marcus finally looked up.

"Tonight didn't go how we wanted," Jack said. "But wanting it never mattered. What matters is what you do next."

He took a breath.

"You want to explain this away, go ahead. Someone else will always listen."

Tyler sat with his forearms on his knees, staring at the floor.

Jack remembered a conversation from earlier in the season, Tyler mentioning his dad almost offhand.

Football's fine, he'd said. *Just don't build your life around it. It'll leave you faster than you think.*

At the time, Jack had nodded. It sounded practical. Safe.

Now, watching Tyler sit there after another loss, Jack wondered what it took for a kid to keep showing up when the people closest to him expected him not to.

No one spoke.

"But if you want to stay," Jack said quietly, "if you want to build something that lasts, then we will find a way."

That was all.

He walked out.

No one cheered.

They didn't need to.

The locker room emptied out in pieces.

Showers hissed down the hall. Lockers slammed once, then less often. Conversations faded until only the low hum of the lights remained.

• • •

Marcus sat at his locker longer than most. Pads still on. Chin strap loose. Staring at the floor like he was replaying something he couldn't rewind.

Neil sat two lockers down, hoodie pulled over his head, helmet at his feet. He wasn't in a hurry either. He never was.

Tyler Briggs finished unlacing his cleats and leaned back against the locker, forearms resting on his knees. He didn't look at either of them when he spoke.

"People think losing is what makes guys leave," he said. His voice stayed low, like it was meant for the room, not the people in it. "It's not."

Marcus didn't look up.

"It's the part after," Tyler continued. "When it stops looking good. When everybody starts telling you it's not worth it."

Marcus swallowed.

"My dad used to say football was a waste if you weren't winning," Tyler said. He picked at a strip of tape on his wrist, slow, deliberate. "Said loyalty was for people who didn't know any better."

Neil shifted slightly but stayed quiet.

"Every time we went 0–10," Tyler went on, "he'd tell me the same thing. Walk away. Nothing's changing. Don't be the idiot who stays."

Tyler finally glanced up, eyes steady.

"So I stayed."

Marcus looked at him now.

"Not because I thought it would turn around fast," Tyler said. "Not because I liked losing. I hated it. Still do."

He shrugged once.

"But if I left too, then he was right. And I wasn't going to give him that."

The room stayed quiet.

Neil watched Tyler's hands. How calm they were. How certain.

Tyler stood and pulled his shirt over his head, movements unhurried.

"Losses hurt," he said. "That's real. But quitting hurts longer."

He grabbed his bag and slung it over his shoulder.

"We find a way," Tyler said, almost like an afterthought. "Or we become what everyone already expects."

He nodded once toward Marcus. Toward Neil. No speech. No challenge.

Then he walked out.

Marcus sat there a moment longer, jaw tight.

Neil didn't move.

Neither of them did.

And for the first time that night, the locker room didn't feel empty.

Marcus stayed seated longer than most.

Cole pulled his jersey over his head and hissed when the fabric caught. Dark bruises bloomed across his ribs and shoulder, finger-shaped, fresh. He reached down and loosened the tape around his ankle, rolled it once, then again. It didn't move the way it should.

Marcus noticed.

"You rolled that early," Marcus said.

First words he'd spoken since the horn.

Cole shrugged. "First quarter."

Marcus shook his head slightly. "You played the whole game on it."

Cole didn't answer. He bent down, retaped tighter, slower this time.

They stood there in the quiet, lockers creaking, showers starting down the hall.

Marcus glanced back at the bruises, then at the ankle.

"I hate that I checked out," he said. "I felt it happening, but couldn't make myself go back in."

Cole straightened, winced, then settled.

"Yeah," he said. Not harsh. Not soft.

Marcus looked up.

Cole met his eyes. No edge. No comfort either.

"We don't get to do that," Cole said. "Not when guys are counting on us."

Marcus swallowed.

"So what do we do?" he asked.

Cole picked up his helmet. His grip tightened when his ankle barked again.

He shrugged.

"We find a way."

• • •

Tyler Briggs stopped on his way out.

Pads still in his hands. Sweat drying on his forearms.

Tyler didn't say much. He never had.

He stood there for a moment, then spoke.

"I'm still with you, Coach."

Jack looked up.

Tyler met his eyes. No speeches. No explanations.

Just loyalty.

Jack nodded once.

It was enough.

• • •

The house was quiet in the way it only got after losses.

Not peaceful.
Just emptied out.

Jack sat at the kitchen table with his laptop open, film paused mid-frame. Cole's jersey, number creased, shoulder pad riding too high, frozen on the screen. Jack had already rewound the same clip three times.

Fourth quarter. Another run. No gain.

"Too upright," Jack muttered. He clicked back five seconds. "You've got to finish that run lower."

Cole sat on the couch with his leg propped up, ice wrapped tight, arms folded. He hadn't said much since they got home. He hadn't complained either. He never did.

Jack rewound again.

"You bounced this," Jack said, tapping the screen, "if you stick it up in there, we're still alive. You've got to trust the crease."

Megan stood in the doorway for a moment before speaking.

"How many carries was that?" she asked.

Jack didn't look up. "Forty-three."

"And how many of those did you just criticize?"

Jack paused the film.

"I'm coaching," he said. Not defensive. Automatic.

Megan walked closer and leaned against the counter. "No," she said calmly. "You're asking for perfection."

Jack turned. "Same thing."

She shook her head. "Not when it's your son."

Silence settled between them.

Jack looked back at the screen. "He knows the standard."

Cole laughed once—short, sharp, humorless.

"That's the problem," he said.

Jack turned fully now. "What problem?"

Cole shifted on the couch, winced as his ankle barked. He ignored it.

"I finished the game," Cole said. His voice was steady, but tight. "On one leg. I didn't tap out. I didn't ask out. I didn't disappear."

Jack nodded. "I know. And I'm proud of—"

"And Marcus quit," Cole cut him off.

The words landed harder than yelling would have.

Jack opened his mouth, then stopped.

Cole sat forward now, elbows on his knees, eyes finally up.

"You didn't rewind his routes," Cole continued. "You didn't freeze the screen on him pulling up. You didn't say anything about him checking out."

Megan stayed quiet. This wasn't hers anymore.

"I'm not mad at him," Cole said. "I get it. He got hit. It happens."

Jack said nothing.

"I'm mad that you don't treat me like him," Cole said. "You never have."

Jack swallowed.

"Because if *I* check out," Cole went on, "it's not just a bad rep. It's 'the coach's kid can't handle it.'"

Silence.

Cole's voice didn't rise. That was the worst part.

"So yeah," he said. "I finished. Because I don't get to be human out there. Not like everyone else."

Jack looked at Megan instinctively.

She met his eyes, but didn't rescue him.

"You ran him into the ground," she said quietly. "And now you're breaking down his mistakes like he failed you."

Jack rubbed his face, elbows on the table now.

"I didn't mean—"

"I know," Megan said. "That doesn't make it okay."

Cole leaned back, exhausted.

"I don't need you to go easy on me," he said. "I just need you to be fair."

Jack stared at the frozen frame on the screen.

Cole's helmet tilted forward.
Leg clearly stiff.
Defender already in the gap.

Jack closed the laptop.
The click sounded final.

"I didn't protect you tonight," he said.

Cole looked at him, surprised.

"I put too much pressure on you," Jack continued. "And I didn't give you many answers."

Megan crossed the room and rested a hand on Jack's shoulder.

"That's coaching too," she said. "Knowing when to protect your boys."

Jack nodded slowly.

After a moment, he looked back at Cole.

"I should've spread the ball out," he said. "Not because you were weak. Because I didn't have a good plan."

Cole didn't smile.
But the tension in his shoulders eased.

"Next time," Cole said quietly, "trust the team to help finish."

Jack nodded.
"I will."

Later, after Cole went to bed, Jack sat alone at the table again. The laptop stayed closed.

He thought about Marcus.

About the difference between fatigue and fear.
About how easy it was to coach toughness—and how hard it was to coach protection.

Megan poured coffee and slid it toward him.

"You can't build men by sacrificing your son," she said.
Jack stared into the cup.

"I know," he said.

And for the first time since the loss, he didn't feel defensive.
He felt corrected.

• • •

The next morning, the call came.

Administration.

Polite. Professional. Careful.

Another assistant had concerns.

Concerns about culture. About discipline. *About softness.*

The meeting was brief.

That night, Megan scrolled her phone longer than usual.

He's in over his head.
Runs his own kid into the ground.
Soft on discipline.

She put the phone down and rubbed her eyes.

Jack noticed.

"You don't have to read that," he said.

She shook her head. "I know. But it still hurts."

Jack nodded.

Some losses bruised bodies.
Others bruised marriages.
All of them tested belief.

And five miles up the road—

West Ridge was still undefeated.

CHAPTER SEVENTEEN

Before He Knew What Stayed

Jack Mercer played for three high schools.

That wasn't a badge of toughness.
It was logistics.

His parents moved when work required it. Sometimes for an opportunity. Sometimes for survival. Always with the same goal, to keep the lights on, keep the family together. They did the best they could. Jack never questioned that.

But moving had consequences.

New hallways.
New coaches.
New expectations.

And every time he started to understand where he fit, it was time to leave.

By the time he was a sophomore, Jack had learned something most kids never had to think about, that belonging was temporary. That lockers changed. That friendships reset. That you could be known somewhere one Friday and invisible somewhere else by Monday morning.

He stopped trying to stand out.

It was easier to stay in the middle. Easier to keep his head down and let seasons pass.

• • •

The second school was different.

Not because of the building.
Because of the coach.

Coach Harlan wasn't loud. Didn't give speeches that lasted forever. Didn't try to be anyone's friend. But he watched everything.

The first week of practice, Jack missed a block during a scrimmage. Not because he didn't know what to do, but because he hesitated.

After practice, Coach Harlan stopped him.

"You're thinking too much," he said.

Jack didn't answer.

Coach Harlan nodded toward the field. "Game moves fast. Decide and go. Even if you're wrong."

That was it.

No lecture. No embarrassment. Just expectation.

Jack noticed something after a few weeks. Coach Harlan knew which kids needed yelling and which ones didn't. He corrected some players in front of everyone. Others, like Jack, he pulled aside quietly.

For the first time in a long time, Jack felt seen without feeling exposed.

That mattered more than he realized at the time.

• • •

That season, Jack played harder than he ever had.

Not for attention.
Not for stats.

Because he didn't want to disappoint that man.

There's a difference.

Jack began staying after practice sometimes, not because he was told to, but because Coach Harlan stayed. Picking up balls. Talking with assistants. Watching film alone in a dark office with the door half open.

One afternoon, Jack lingered near the doorway, watching film play silently on the screen.

Coach Harlan didn't look up.
"Sit down if you're going to stand there," he said.

Jack sat.

They watched two drives without speaking.

Finally, Jack asked, "How do you see all that?"

Coach Harlan shrugged. "You just keep watching."

Jack didn't realize it then, but something shifted in that moment. Not dramatic. Not loud. Just a quiet awareness that there was a way to live inside the game that wasn't about being the one holding the ball.

He started watching differently after that.
Not just his assignment. Everyone's.

He didn't know it yet, but that was the first time he thought, without quite naming it, that he might want to coach someday.

• • •

Then they moved again.

And just like that, it was over.

No closure.
Just a handshake in the parking lot.

"Keep working," Coach Harlan told him.

Jack nodded.

He never saw him again.

But he never forgot him either.

• • •

The third school felt like starting over in a place that already had its own story.

By then, Jack was tired of being the new kid.

He was good at football, good enough to matter, not good enough to be untouchable. All-conference. Tough. Reliable. The kind of player coaches trusted on Friday nights.

But he wasn't a college prospect.

No recruiters calling. No scholarship letters taped to the fridge. Football kept him visible, not secure.

During his senior year, his parents moved again.

Jack didn't.

Not because of rebellion. Because of exhaustion.

He stayed with friends. Different couches. Different kitchens. Families who did their best to pretend this was temporary.

It was stable enough.

And unstable enough to matter.

Some mornings, he woke up before everyone else and sat on the edge of a couch, listening to a house that wasn't his wake up around him, coffee brewing, cabinets opening, footsteps on hardwood floors. He learned how to move quietly in other people's homes. How to leave early. How not to be in the way.

He kept his duffel bag zipped most of the time.

It was easier that way.

Easier to leave.

• • •

With no one really watching, Jack learned something dangerous: that poor decisions didn't always demand an immediate response.

He wasn't a bad kid.

He showed up to practice. Passed just enough classes. Never caused real trouble. He was respectful when adults were around.

But he drifted.

And drifting is hardest on people who haven't learned how to stop themselves.

Late nights. Wrong crowds. Anger without direction. Confidence without grounding.

Sports were the only thing that kept him tethered to school. Practice gave structure. Games gave purpose. Coaches gave expectations he didn't yet know how to give himself.

When the season ended, the tether loosened.

College came without ceremony. He managed to get accepted and enrolled, and that was about it.

No send-off. No sense of arrival. Just a duffel bag and the quiet understanding that football wasn't following him this time.

• • •

Stability didn't arrive loudly.

That was when he met Megan.

Not in a dramatic way. Not a movie moment.

She sat next to him in a class he almost dropped.

She noticed him before he noticed himself.

She asked questions that assumed he had answers. She expected him to show up. She didn't laugh at his excuses and didn't argue with them either.

She just waited.

Megan didn't rescue him.

She didn't need to.

She believed he could be better before he had any proof.

One afternoon, he showed up late to class and slid into the seat beside her like it didn't matter.

She looked at him and said quietly, "You're better than that."

Not angry.
Not disappointed.
Just certain.

It bothered him the rest of the day.

Not because she was wrong.
Because she was right.

For the first time, Jack felt something unfamiliar.

Accountability that wasn't enforced, but didn't move.
Stability that wasn't temporary.
Grace that didn't remove standards.

And he wanted to be the person who would live up to those standards.

He started going to class more. Sleeping better. Thinking longer than the next weekend.

The version of Jack that drifted didn't disappear overnight.

But it stopped being the one in charge.

• • •

Years later, standing in locker rooms and kitchens and quiet offices, Jack would think back to that time, not with regret, but understanding.

He understood now what he hadn't then.

Kids don't need perfection.
They need presence.

They don't need someone to save them.
They need someone who stays long enough to expect more.

Jack didn't know it yet, but everything he would build later traced back to that season of instability, the coach who saw him before he saw himself, and the one person who refused to let him drift without asking for more.

That was where it started,
long before he had a whistle.

CHAPTER EIGHTEEN

What You Do After Losing

Marcus didn't talk much on the Monday after the conference loss.

He showed up early. Helmet buckled. Eyes forward.

But the looseness was gone.

Jack noticed it during warm-ups. The extra stiffness in Marcus's shoulders, the way he caught the ball like it might bite him, the way he drifted to the back of the lines instead of the front.

Fear didn't announce itself.

It just took small pieces.

Last year, Jack would've said something right away. Pulled him aside. Demanded more. Tried to fix it.

That version of him cared too much about the next result.

Jack didn't single Marcus out. Didn't pull him aside. Didn't tell him he needed to be tougher.

He changed the work.

Jack stopped practice.

Not angry. Just done.

He pointed to the drill line.

"If you need me watching you to do it right," he said, "you don't get it yet."

No one moved.

"Standards don't work when they need supervision," he said. "They work when they're yours."

He blew the whistle.

"Again."

That week's team theme went up Tuesday morning.

Jack wrote it slowly, deliberately.

ANSWER

Under it, a line he'd carried long before Iron Valley:

Adversity doesn't define a program. How you answer—when there's no easy way—does.

No explanation.
No sermon.

They practiced fundamentals like the scoreboard didn't exist. Routes on air. Blocking angles. Tackling fits. Reps without pressure. Teaching without urgency.

The difference showed up immediately.

Last season, a loss had tightened everyone up. Coaches louder. Players quieter. Everyone feeling like the next mistake might cost them everything.

This time, the kids leaned in.

They trusted the work.

Marcus stayed after practice.

Not because he was asked.

Because he needed it.

Coach Evans stayed too.

They didn't talk about the hits. They talked about footwork. Hand placement. Eyes. Evans corrected calmly, deliberately.

Marcus caught every ball thrown to him.

Slowly.

Confidence returned the way it always did.

Quietly.

Tyler Briggs noticed.

He started pulling younger linemen aside between reps. Not to lecture. Just to steady them.

"Next one," he'd say.
"Finish it."

Guys listened.

Jack caught Marcus just outside the locker room.

Not angry.
Not loud.
Just there.

"Walk with me," Jack said.

They moved down the sideline while the rest of the team filtered out. Stadium lights hummed above them. Grass still warm under their cleats.

Jack stopped near the numbers.

"You know why I'm harder on you than most," he said.

Marcus stared at the turf. "Because I messed up?"

Jack shook his head. "Because you matter."

Marcus looked up.

Jack took a breath. "Let me tell you something nobody told me soon enough."

He waited until Marcus met his eyes.

"The difference between a boy and a man," Jack said, "is that a boy does what he wants to do all the time and a man does what has to be done."

Marcus swallowed.

"Boys choose the easy path," Jack continued. "And easy doesn't build anything."

Marcus nodded slowly.

"I don't need you perfect," Jack said. "I need you dependable. I need you to show up when it's uncomfortable. When nobody's clapping. When it would be easier to disappear."

Jack stepped back.

"You didn't choose your situation," he said quietly. "But how you respond to it means everything."

Marcus didn't say anything.

He just nodded once and jogged back toward the locker room.

Jack watched him go.

• • •

Friday night came again.

Another solid opponent. Older. Physical. Well-coached.

Jack felt the familiar knot in his stomach. This team wouldn't beat itself either.

But something was different from the first snap.

Jack spread it out early.

Not flashy. Not experimental. Just deliberate.

First series:
Quick game.
Swing to the back.
A hitch to Marcus.
Inside zone with the backup tailback rotating in.

Cole handed the ball off and jogged back to the huddle without comment.

Second series:
Play-action.
Tight end leak.
Receiver screen.

The ball moved. Not fast. Not explosive. But steady.

Cole didn't press. Didn't try to make something happen that wasn't there. He ran what was called. Threw where it was supposed to go. Took what the defense offered and nothing more.

On the sideline, Jack felt it immediately.

The questions would come later.
Why aren't you feeding him?
Why change what works?

But this wasn't about what worked last week.

This was about what lasted.

By the end of the first quarter, Cole had touched the ball four times.

That would've been unthinkable a month ago.

Early in the second quarter, Marcus took a hit.

Not the kind that rattled helmets, but the kind that tested resolve.

He popped up and jogged back to the huddle.

Cole slapped his helmet once. Tyler clapped from the sideline.

Jack exhaled.

Marcus caught a touchdown late in the third quarter. Not a deep ball. A dig route. Traffic. Contact.

Midway through the third quarter, the game tightened.

Iron Valley clung to a four-point lead. The offense stalled twice. The crowd shifted in their seats, restless.

Cole stood beside Jack on the sideline, helmet tucked under his arm. Sweat ran down the side of his face. He watched the defense jog back on, hands on hips.

Jack didn't look at him.

He didn't need to.

Cole spoke first.

"I'm good," he said.

Jack glanced over.

Not rushed. Not defensive.

"I know," Jack said.

Cole hesitated. Then nodded toward the field.

"They're starting to widen," he said. "Backers are slow to fit."

Jack watched the replay board. Saw it now. Half a step late. Overplaying the perimeter.

"You want it?" Jack asked.

Cole didn't answer right away.

He took a breath.

"Yeah," he said. "I want it."

Not demanding.
Not emotional.
Certain.

Jack nodded once.

"Alright," he said. "We'll lean on you."

Cole pulled his helmet on and jogged toward the huddle.

The next drive looked different.

Power.
Counter.
Inside zone.

Cole ran behind Tyler and didn't bounce it. Lowered his pads. Finished forward.

Six yards.
Four.
Five.

Nothing spectacular.

But the defense felt it.

Late in the fourth quarter, Iron Valley chewed clock.

Iron Valley won by one score.

Clean. Earned.

No fireworks.
No miracle.

Just control.

In the locker room, Jack didn't say much.

He didn't need to.

Cole sat on the bench, unlacing his cleats. Tired. Bruised. Still standing.

Jack stopped beside him.

"Good job," he said.

Cole nodded. "Thanks for trusting me."

Jack met his eyes.

"Thanks for trusting me back."

That was it.

• • •

The win was celebrated, and then the news broke.

"4–1 in conference," Jack said once the noise died. "That's all."

The kids nodded.

They understood now.

Especially when someone checked their phone.

West Ridge had beaten Central Heights.

The same Central Heights team Iron Valley had gone toe-to-toe with.

The math didn't need explaining.

Conference standings tightened.
Possibilities whispered.

Week 9 stopped being hypothetical.

Five miles.

Later that night, Jack sat alone in his office, lights low, film paused on a simple inside zone run that had gone for eight yards.

Nothing special.

Perfect execution.

This is executing, he thought.

Not luck.
Not emotion.

Work.

Megan texted him from home:

House full again.

Jack smiled.

Iron Valley was 4–1 in conference.

The rival was 5–0 in conference.

They were on a collision course now.

• • •

That night, the house was filled.

The yard buzzed with conversation, the steady rhythm of people eating and talking at the same time. Foil crinkled as leftovers were passed around. A cooler lid slammed somewhere near the fence. Megan moved through the crowd quietly, checking on people, refilling drinks, and listening more than she spoke.

Neil sat with Cole and a couple of linemen, laughing so hard he had to wipe his eyes, the sound carrying across the table.

Marcus sat nearby.

Quiet as usual. Hoodie sleeves pulled down over his hands. He ate carefully, slower than the others, like he wasn't sure how long it would last.

Megan noticed.

She always did.

She slid another plate toward him without saying anything. Later, she quietly packed him extra food "for tomorrow," like it was no big deal.

Jack watched from the porch.

Did I make the right call?
Was I too patient? Too soft?

The questions hadn't left him since Ray walked out.

Megan sat beside him.

"They trust you," she said.

Jack nodded.

Inside, a group of seniors cornered him near the door. Tyler stood with them, arms crossed, eyes steady.

"Coach," one of them said, "we need to say something."

Jack waited.

"We've lost before," another added. "A lot." With a slight laugh.

Jack nodded and smiled.

"But when we lost back then," the first continued, "it always felt like that's all coaches saw."

Silence settled in.

"This time," the kid said, "you didn't leave us there."

Jack felt his chest tighten.

"You didn't act like we were losers," another senior said. "You kept building us."

Tyler finally spoke.

"We are glad you are our coach," he said simply.

Jack searched for words.

He didn't find any.

Later, when the house finally quieted and the lights went out one by one, Jack sat alone at the kitchen table.

He thought about Marcus.
About Tyler stepping into leadership without being asked.
About Neil sitting quietly, grateful for a place to belong.
About the assistant he'd let go.
About Cole carrying the weight he hadn't chosen yet.

This mattered, he realized.

Not the wins.
Not the praise.
Not the noise.

The response.

He wasn't shocked by doubt.

He was shocked by trust.

CHAPTER NINETEEN

Redemption Has a Name

Jack didn't plan to tell that story.

He never did.

The word was already on the board before he could talk himself out of it.

REDEMPTION

The room stayed still longer than usual.

Not the awkward kind of stillness.
The kind that presses in.

Jack stood there with the marker still in his hand, feeling the weight of it settle into the room—and into himself. This wasn't a word you tossed around casually. Not if you meant it. Not if you understood what it cost.

He capped the marker and turned to the team.

"This one's mine," he said.

A few heads lifted. A few eyes sharpened.

"I don't coach because football saved me," Jack continued. "Football didn't."

Silence.

"I coach because someone did."

Jack leaned back against the whiteboard, arms crossed, not defensive, just steady. Grounded. He didn't pace. He didn't fill the space.

"When I was your age, I wasn't impressive," he said. "Not as a player. Not as a student. Definitely not as a person."

He paused, letting the words find their place.

"I made choices that should've closed doors."

The room was quiet enough to hear lockers creak. Somewhere, someone shifted their feet and stopped.

"I was angry," Jack said. "Aimless. Thought I knew more than everyone around me."

A faint, almost embarrassed shake of his head.

"I didn't."

He took a breath. Longer this time.

"I met my wife when I was that guy."

A few smiles flickered. Megan's name carried weight here now; she'd earned that without ever asking for it.

"She didn't fix me," Jack said. "That's important."

He let that sentence breathe.

"She didn't excuse me either."

Jack glanced down for a moment, then back up.

"She held a standard I wasn't meeting. And when I failed, she didn't walk away, but she didn't lower it."

A swallow moved through the room.

"I had people who expected me to become exactly what my choices were pointing toward," Jack continued. "She expected more."

He let the silence do its work.

"I'm here because she redeemed me when I didn't deserve it," Jack said. "She made me a better man before I ever tried to be a good coach."

He straightened slightly.

"That's why I coach the way I do," he said. "Because someone believed I was more than my worst season."

He turned back to the board, then faced them again.

"So now I'm asking you."

The room tensed, not with fear, but vulnerability.

"Who helped redeem you?"

No one spoke.

Jack nodded. "Take a minute."

He stepped aside.

Silence stretched.

It always did the work better than he could.

A senior raised his hand halfway… then dropped it.

Another stared at the floor, jaw tight.

Then Marcus stood.

His mouth opened once, then closed. His hands hung at his sides and his fingers curled into loose fists, then uncurled again. He looked at Jack like he was asking permission for something Jack hadn't offered.

Jack gave the smallest nod.

Marcus swallowed.

Not slowly.
Not dramatically.

He just stood.

Jack felt the room lean forward.

"My mom," Marcus said.

A few heads turned. A few eyebrows lifted, not with judgment, just surprise.

"She wasn't always like this," Marcus continued quietly. "There was a time… it was bad."

He paused, jaw tightening as if holding something in place.

"No food sometimes. No lights. People coming in and out."
He swallowed.

"I slept in my shoes because sometimes I didn't know if I'd have to go pick her up some nights. I'd wake up to sirens and wonder if she was coming back that night."

The room stayed completely still now.

"Football practice," Marcus said, voice steady but softer, "was the only place the noise stopped."

No one moved.

"One night," Marcus continued, "I woke up and she was gone. For real gone. Nobody knew where."

Jack didn't move.

"She came back weeks later," Marcus said. "Different. Clean. Quiet."

Marcus lifted his eyes now. Wet, but steady.

"She didn't apologize much," he said. "She just stayed."

A breath moved through the room.

"And I stayed too."

Stillness.

"She hasn't even figured out how to make herself well," Marcus finished. "But she does all she can to make sure I have all she can give."

The silence that followed wasn't awkward.
It was sacred.

Neil, who had been staring at the floor, slowly looked up. Understanding in a way that kids his age rarely did.

Cole sat back in his chair, eyes on Marcus, the way quarterbacks watch receivers after they finally understand where they're supposed to be. Something in his expression had changed, not sympathy, not pity. Respect.

Along the wall, two of the older players who had quietly blamed Marcus for Ray leaving shifted where they sat. One of them rubbed the back of his neck. The other looked down at his hands, then back at Marcus again, like he was seeing him for the first time.

Nobody said anything.

Coach Evans wiped his face with his sleeve and stared hard at the floor. A lineman leaned forward, elbows on his knees, hands shaking slightly.

Jack cleared his throat.

"That's redemption," he said softly. "Not erasing the past. Redeeming the future."

No one moved right away.

But something in the room had changed.

And everyone felt it.

He looked around the room.

"You're not changing this program alone," Jack said. "You're changing each other."

No cheers.
No clapping.

Just understanding.

• • •

After practice, the field felt different. Players lingered longer. Talked more honestly. Listened better. Corrections landed softer. Effort felt purposeful, not forced.

Marcus sat on the bench, helmet on the ground between his feet.

"I don't know how to deal with all this," he said.

Jack didn't correct him.

Didn't rush him.

"I didn't say it'd be clean," Jack replied. "Or easy."

Marcus looked up.

"I said we try to figure it out together."

Marcus nodded slowly.

Not because he felt better.

Because he felt seen.

Marcus sat there a while longer, rolling the football between his palms.

"She's been home every night for almost two months," he said quietly. "Dylan's been sleeping in his own room again. Not the couch."

He looked at Jack.

"I think she's actually trying this time."

Jack nodded.

He didn't say what he was thinking, that hope was the most dangerous thing a kid like Marcus could carry, because it was also the only thing worth holding onto.

That night, the house filled again.

Megan moved through the kitchen like she always did, feeding, listening, noticing. She caught Jack watching her and smiled.

"What?" she asked.

Jack shook his head. "Just… thank you."

She nodded.

No words needed.

Jack stood in the doorway, listening to laughter fade into the night.

Marcus was still in the kitchen, rinsing a plate that didn't belong to him.

Megan dried it and set it back in the cabinet without saying a word.

Jack watched them a moment longer, then turned off the light.

Redemption didn't show up in wins.
Didn't live on highlight tapes.

It lived here.

CHAPTER TWENTY

Ordinary Feels Good

The next day's practice was one of the best they'd had all season.

Not because it was loud.
Not because it was perfect.

Because it was clean.

The first whistle blew and the rhythm felt right immediately. Players moved from drill to drill without coaches pushing them. Helmets were down, feet were active, corrections happened in short sentences instead of long speeches. The air carried that quiet hum of a group that understood what it was supposed to do.

Jack stood near the numbers, hands on his hips, watching inside run.

Tyler finished a block and jogged back to the huddle already talking to the younger lineman beside him, pointing at the defensive front and explaining something quietly. Not just correcting, but teaching.

Cole took the next rep, made the read, handed the ball off, and jogged back without looking to the sideline for approval.

Marcus hit the right landmark on the next play without hesitation, catching the ball and getting north, finishing the run without celebration.

No one was trying to impress anyone.

They were just working.

Jack realized he hadn't raised his voice in nearly fifteen minutes.

He found himself smiling without meaning to.

Sometimes the best practices were the quietest ones.

Practice ended with conditioning that didn't feel like punishment and a team period that moved quickly, the last rep ending with a whistle that echoed across the field as the sun dipped lower behind the stands.

Players began drifting toward the locker room in small groups, shoulder pads hanging loose, conversation low and easy.

Cole sat on a bench near the sideline, peeling tape from his wrists. Neil stood nearby, helmet hanging from one hand, talking quietly about something they'd seen in team period.

A truck rolled slowly into the parking lot.

Neil glanced up.

"There's my dad," he said.

Jack was crossing the field toward the equipment shed when the truck door opened. Neil's father stepped out, work boots dusty, shoulders carrying the kind of fatigue that came from long hours and not enough rest, but he was smiling as he walked toward them.

"Coach," he said, offering his hand.

Jack shook it. "Good to see you."

"How's he doing?" his dad asked, nodding toward Neil.

Jack looked at Neil for a moment before answering.

"He's doing well," Jack said. "Very bright kid. Sees the game well. He's maximizing what he's got, and that's what good players do."

Neil looked down slightly, not embarrassed, just absorbing it.

His dad nodded, pride showing in the small ways fathers try to hide it.

"I appreciate that, Coach," he said.

Neil picked up his bag.

They started walking toward the truck together.

As they reached it, Jack heard his dad say quietly, "I'm proud of you."

Neil didn't answer right away.

Then he nodded once.

Cole stood a few steps back, silent, watching, not intruding, just present.

The truck pulled out of the lot a minute later, taillights fading as it turned onto the road.

The field grew quiet again.

Jack stood there a moment longer, listening to the wind move lightly across the grass, then turned toward the field house.

• • •

That afternoon, Jack walked to Bennett's youth practice.

Partly to watch his son.

Partly because he knew Marcus would be there.

The youth teams practiced on the smaller field beside the middle school, where the grass was thinner, and the yard lines weren't always straight. Cones marked boundaries. Parents sat in folding chairs along the sideline. Coaches crouched low, talking in calm voices that sounded bigger to kids than they meant to.

Bennett was at linebacker, crouched low, eyes serious, taking every rep like it mattered.

Jack watched for a few minutes, letting himself just be a dad, not a coach.

Then he looked across the field.

Marcus stood near the sideline watching Dylan run drills.

Hands in his pockets. Quiet. Relaxed in a way Jack rarely saw at high school practice.

Jack started to walk over.

Then he stopped.

Tyler was already there.

And two other seniors.

They stood beside Marcus talking about something small, nothing important, just a normal conversation. Dylan jogged past them once and Marcus reached out, tapping his helmet lightly, saying something that made Dylan grin.

Tyler laughed at whatever Marcus said next.

Jack watched them for a moment.

No one was performing.
No one was trying to impress anyone.

Just players standing together on the sideline, talking like they belonged to the same world.

Jack realized Marcus didn't need him right now.

That mattered more than he expected.

He turned back toward Bennett's practice, folding his arms along the fence, watching his son shuffle sideways through a drill, trying to stay in front of a running back who was determined to bounce everything outside.

The sun dropped lower, the light softening, shadows stretching across the field.

Parents began gathering equipment. Kids chased loose footballs. Coaches blew final whistles that no one really hurried to obey.

Jack stood there a few minutes longer, breathing in the quiet, the ordinary rhythm of a day that didn't feel important while it was happening.

• • •

Later, as he walked back to his truck, he looked once more at the field.

The season had settled into a rhythm now.

Practice.
School.
Film.
Lifting.

Laughing in the locker room.
Players lingered longer than they needed to.

Normal things.

Things that didn't feel important while they were happening.

But were.

For the first time in a long time, the program felt steady.

Not perfect.
Not finished.

But steady.

Jack got into his truck and sat there a moment before starting it, watching the last of the kids leave the field, their voices carrying faintly across the evening air. Bennett jumped in as they headed home.

Sometimes the most ordinary days are the ones you remember later.

CHAPTER TWENTY-ONE

Some Things Don't Heal by Winning

The call came during fourth period.

Jack knew before he answered it that nothing good ever came from calls like that. Not in the middle of a school day. Not when the voice on the other end already sounded nervous.

The counselor didn't waste words.

"There's been an accident," she said. "One of our players."

Jack closed his eyes.

The counselor kept talking, but Jack didn't hear most of it.

The hallway noise blurred together: footsteps, lockers, a voice calling from down the hall. It all sounded far away, like it was happening in another building.

Jack stared at a scuff mark on the floor near the desk and realized he'd been looking at it for several seconds without blinking.

A parent. Gone.

Just like that.

Jack's next breath caught high in his chest like a hook. The counselor's voice kept going, but the words flattened into static. His free hand found the edge of the desk; fingers pressed until the wood creaked.
By the time Jack reached the locker room, the team already knew. Word moved faster than facts; half-truths, whispers, and silence filled in the gaps.

Neil Parker sat alone.

He sat on the bench staring at the same spot on the floor, like something had been written there that only he could see.

Someone spoke to him once. Then again.

He didn't answer.

His hands rested on his knees, fists tightening slowly, then loosening, then tightening again, like his body didn't know what to do with itself.

Neil had always been *around*, close to Marcus, closer to Cole, but never the center of anything.

Until now.

Jack walked over and sat beside him.

"I'm here," Jack said.

Neil nodded, eyes fixed on the floor, as if he looked up, something worse might happen.

"My dad was supposed to pick me up today," Neil said quietly.

Jack felt the air leave his lungs.

Neil wasn't crying.

That scared him.

Practice was canceled.

• • •

Some assistants looked confused. Others relieved. Jack didn't explain. There wasn't anything to explain. There was no blueprint for how to handle this.

That night, the house filled again, but differently.

Megan cooked without music. The house felt smaller. The laughter that usually spilled into the yard stayed trapped in the kitchen. It got even quieter when Neil arrived.

Neil sat at the table with Marcus and Cole. His plate sat untouched.

Marcus tried once.

"You want something else?" he asked.

Neil shook his head.

Cole leaned back in his chair, staring at the ceiling like he was trying to find the right words. He didn't find them.

None of them did.

Neil didn't cry.

Marcus watched him too closely. Cole watched him too quietly.

The next morning, Jack wrote the Team Theme on the board before anyone arrived.

He wrote it larger than usual.

RESILIENCE

Under it, he wrote a line he hadn't planned to share, one he'd written years ago and never thought he'd say out loud again:

'Resilience isn't about bouncing back.
It's about standing when you don't want to."

When the team gathered, Jack didn't pace.

He stayed still.

"This week isn't about football," he said. "But football will be here anyway."

He looked directly at Neil.

"You don't owe us strength," Jack said. "You don't owe us anything. If you need to be away, our team will support you."

Neil nodded once.

"We'll play on Friday," Jack continued. "Not because it matters more than this, but because sometimes structure is the only thing holding people up."

No one argued.

• • •

Neil was not at school for the next few days.

Wednesday practice felt off.

Not loud. Not sloppy. Just incomplete.

A few drills dragged longer than they should have. Periods ended without the usual energy. Coaches corrected things twice that normally only needed to be said once.

They felt like they were at work instead of playing a game.

It wasn't effort they were missing.

It was presence.

And everyone knew why.

• • •

Friday night arrived like it always did.

Lights on.
Bands playing.
Announcers talking.

But something was missing.

When Neil walked into the locker room before pregame, conversation faded.

Not all at once.
One voice at a time.

A few players looked up from taping ankles. One helmet stopped mid-snap. The music from someone's phone kept playing for a few seconds before someone quietly turned it off.

Neil didn't say anything.
Didn't make eye contact.

He walked to his locker, sat down, and began taping his wrists like it was any other Friday.

The sound of the tape pulling tight echoed softly in the room.

Tyler looked at Jack.

Jack nodded once.

No one made a speech.

But everyone understood.

• • •

Iron Valley played well. Efficient. Disciplined. Focused. Cole ran hard, too hard at times.

Marcus caught everything thrown his way but didn't celebrate a single one.

Late in the second quarter, Cole kept the ball on a read and broke into the open field.

He ran harder than Jack had seen him run all season, arms pumping, jaw tight, finishing through contact even when he didn't need to.

When the whistle blew, Cole handed the ball to the official and turned away quickly.

Jack saw him wipe his face with his wrist as he jogged back to the huddle.

He wasn't celebrating.

He was carrying something.

Tyler looked like a madman out there blocking. But after each block, he would almost walk exhausted back to the huddle.

Neil had asked to dress and played a few plays on special teams. When the game got out of hand, Jack put him in for the last two drives on defense. When he made a tackle, the entire sideline erupted, and so did the crowd.

Jack caught himself choking up and quickly wiped his face, then joined in the cheers for Neil.

Jack couldn't look at the stands, but he knew where Neil's mom would be, right next to Megan.

They won.

Comfortably.

The horn sounded.

No helmets flew.
No music played.

After the handshake line, Neil stared straight ahead and walked off the field through tears he didn't bother hiding.

Marcus followed without saying anything. Cole trailed behind them, jaw tight, eyes glassy.

In the locker room, helmets came off quietly. Shoulder pads unclipped. No one rushed.

Jack thought about Marcus standing in front of the team weeks earlier, talking about staying when things were hard.

Some lessons didn't show up in drills.

They showed up here.

And now he couldn't even look at Neil without his throat tightening up.

Jack didn't say much. What was there to say in moments like this?

"I'm proud of you guys," Jack said quietly.

He looked toward Neil.

"You showed us something tonight that most people never get to see. I know your father would be proud."

• • •

Later that night, Jack sat on the porch steps, elbows on his knees, staring into the dark.

Megan sat beside him without speaking.

For a long time, neither of them said anything.

"Neil made that tackle and the whole place went crazy," Jack said finally, voice rough. "And all I could think was, his dad should be in those stands right now. Not me. Not the crowd. His dad."

Megan didn't answer right away.

Jack rubbed his face hard with both hands, and when he lowered them, his eyes were wet. He didn't try to hide it.

"What a great kid," he said quietly, "I can't imagine what he is going through right now."

Megan reached for his hand.

"You're not able to protect them from everything," she said softly. "Just help them stand when it comes."

"What if football is just something I hide behind?" he continued. "What if it's just a distraction I dressed up as purpose, and these kids are carrying real weight that no team theme or Friday night is ever going to touch?"

Megan sat beside him.

"Then you still showed up," she said. "And so did they."

Jack stared out into the dark.

He thought about Neil, sitting in that locker room with more questions than answers.

About Marcus, hurting for someone else in a way he didn't know how to fix.

About Cole, learning that leadership sometimes meant carrying grief that wasn't yours.

Football couldn't fix that.

But it could hold them up long enough to breathe.

Jack pulled the blanket tighter around his shoulders.

Week 9 was coming.

But for the first time, he wasn't thinking about rivals or records.

He was thinking about his impact on these kids.

And whether showing up, again and again, was enough.

For the first time, he believed it might be.

CHAPTER TWENTY-TWO

Showing Up Still Counts

Neil didn't come to school on Monday.

Jack knew why before anyone said it out loud.

The funeral was that morning.

The team went together. No announcement. No speech about unity. Just a quiet understanding that this was where they were supposed to be.

The players arrived in small groups, jackets borrowed, ties crooked, dress shoes that hadn't seen much use.

They filled the rows behind Jack and Megan, sitting straighter than usual, unsure where to put their hands or their eyes.

One kid kept adjusting a too-big collar. Another stared down at the folded program in his hands like it might tell him what to do next.

No one talked much.

Neil sat in the front with the family.

He didn't look back.

Jack was glad for that.

Some moments weren't meant to be shared across a room.

Practice was canceled that afternoon.

Not postponed.
Canceled.

No one questioned it.

• • •

The school weight room smelled like rubber mats and old sweat—the same way it always did when no one else was supposed to be there.

Neil had the key from Coach Evans.

It had been handed to him without a speech the day after the funeral. Just a nod.

"Use it when you need to."

He didn't turn on the overhead lights.

The red glow from the exit sign was enough: benches, racks, iron plates stacked along the wall. He didn't want brightness. Brightness asked questions.

He sat on the edge of the bench press, still in the black dress pants and white shirt from earlier. Sleeves rolled once. Tie gone. Shoes off. Socks flat against the cold floor.

The bar waited in the rack.

He slid it out and felt the familiar pull settle into his hands. Enough weight to work. Enough to breathe.

First set. Bench press.

Slow. Controlled.

He breathed out on the way up, the way Coach Mercer taught in form drills. The bar moved clean. No shake. No rush.

He racked it. Sat up. Elbows on his knees. Stared at the space between his feet.

The funeral came back in pieces. The preacher's voice too loud for the size of the room. His mom's hand gripping his until it hurt. Teammates not knowing what to say to him.

Marcus had stayed beside him the whole time.
Cole too.
No one talked much. No one needed to.

Neil stood.

Power cleans next.

He set his feet. Gripped the bar. Pulled.
The bar came up smooth to his shoulders. Down again.
Again.

Same rhythm. No rush. No noise.

He stopped after ten. Racked the bar. Walked to the water fountain, not because he was thirsty, but because moving felt better than standing still. The water tasted metallic. Cold. He swallowed once and let the rest run into the drain.

Back to the rack.

Squats.

The bar settled across his shoulders. Down slow. Knees tracking. Chest up. He held at the bottom for two seconds.

Nobody watching.

Up. Breathe. Down again.

He didn't count reps. He just kept moving until his legs remembered they were still here. Still working. Still his.

Eventually, he sat on the floor, back against the wall, knees pulled in. Sweat darkened his sleeves. The red exit light caught the damp shine on his forearms.

Under the dress shirt, he wore his dad's old flannel, the one his dad used to wear to games when Neil was younger. He wiped his arms with it and left it there.

He didn't cry.

Not here.

Crying would mean letting go of the control he was holding onto. The bar was control. The reps were control. The quiet was control.

He looked up at the far wall where the FIND A WAY sign hung. The fresh paint clashed with all the old weight equipment.

Neil closed his eyes.

He thought about his dad's laugh, the short one he saved for when Neil made a good read in practice. He thought about the accident. He thought about the hospital room. The beeping. The way his dad's hand had gone still.

When he opened his eyes, the clock on the wall read 2:47.

Practice would start at 6:30.

He'd be back then.
Different clothes. Different face.
Same kid.

Neil stood. Slid the bar back into the rack. Headed for the exit.

The red exit sign stayed on.

He locked the door behind him.

Outside, the afternoon air bit just enough to wake him up. He didn't hurry to the truck.

He just walked.

One step. Then another.

Finding a way.

Even when the way felt empty.

• • •

Tuesday, Neil came back.

No announcement.
No heads-up.
No explanation.

Jack saw him from his office window, walking across the practice field in jeans and a hoodie, hands shoved into his pockets like he wasn't sure where they belonged anymore.

Jack didn't go meet him right away.

That was the hardest part.

He'd learned over time that rushing grief usually made it retreat deeper, not disappear. So he waited. Let Neil find his way into the building on his own.

Neil stood just inside the locker room door for a long moment, watching the team move around him. Helmets clanked. Someone laughed. Someone cursed after dropping a roll of tape.

Life, still moving.

Finally, Neil stepped in.

Practice slowed without anyone saying anything. A few players nodded. A few clapped him on the shoulder as they passed. Nobody asked questions.

Good, Jack thought.
They're learning.

Neil dressed but didn't fully gear up. Jack didn't ask him to. He let him stand with the linebackers, let him listen, let him feel normal without being forced into it.

Marcus drifted over at one point. Didn't say much. Just stood next to him.

Cole followed later. Helmet in hand. Same quiet presence.

Neil noticed.

That mattered.

After practice, Neil waited.

Jack spotted him sitting on the bench, helmet resting in his lap, eyes fixed on the floor like it might offer answers.

"Walk with me," Jack said.

They went out onto the field, grass damp under their feet. The stadium was empty—quiet in a way it rarely was anymore.

"I don't know if I'm ready," Neil said suddenly. "I don't even know what ready means."

Jack nodded. "You don't have to know."

Neil swallowed. "I just didn't want to stay home."

Jack stopped walking.

"That's enough," he said. "That's more than enough."

That night, Jack didn't go straight home.

He drove past the school, past the stadium, and pulled over on a side road where the lights didn't reach. He sat in the truck with the engine off, hands resting on the steering wheel.

He didn't know how to start.

He rarely prayed out loud, but didn't know what else to do.

"Okay," he finally said aloud. "I don't know what I'm doing here."

Silence answered back.

"I keep telling them football isn't everything," Jack continued. "But I built my life around it."

He exhaled.

"I don't know how to help kids when I can't fix anything that actually hurts."

He rested his forehead against the wheel.

"I don't care about winning," he said quietly. "I just need to know this matters."

The words felt small when they left his mouth.

Jack sat there longer than he planned. When he finally turned the key and drove home, nothing felt resolved, but something felt steadier.

• • •

Marcus didn't come to practice the next day.

Jack knew before anyone told him.

Coach Evans found him after school.

"Marcus's mom relapsed again," Evans said. "He's with his aunt for now."

Jack nodded, jaw tight.

"How bad?" Jack asked.

Evans shook his head slowly. "Bad enough that the aunt came and got them both from the house."

Jack stared at the whiteboard behind Evans for a long time without reading any of it.

Patterns had a way of repeating themselves when you weren't ready.

• • •

The knock came after eight.

Megan opened the door and found Marcus standing on the porch with Dylan half-asleep against his side. Dylan's backpack hung off one shoulder, unzipped, a corner of notebook paper sticking out.

Marcus didn't say anything at first. His jaw was set and his eyes were red, but dry, like the crying had already happened somewhere else and he'd walked through the rest of it to get here.

"Come in," Megan said.

She didn't ask why.

Dylan shuffled to the couch and curled up immediately. Cole came out of the hallway, saw the situation, grabbed a blanket from the closet, and draped it over Dylan without a word. Then he sat on the other end of the couch, turned on the television low, and stayed.

Jack was still at the school. Megan didn't call him.

She made a plate. Chicken, rice, green beans. She set it in front of Marcus at the kitchen table and poured herself a glass of water and sat across from him.

Marcus picked up the fork and put it back down.

"She told me she was done with it," he said. His voice was flat. Not sad. Not yet. Just flat, the way a voice sounds when it's been carrying too much and finally gives out under thc weight.

Megan didn't respond right away.

"She looked me in the face," Marcus continued. "Three weeks ago. Sat on the edge of my bed and told me it was over."

He pressed his thumb hard against the edge of the table.

"I told the whole team about her. I stood up in front of everybody and told them what she put us through, and I said she stayed. I said she was trying."

His voice cracked on the last word.

"And she couldn't even make it to Thanksgiving."

The kitchen was quiet except for the low hum of the television in the other room.

Megan let the silence sit. She didn't fill it. Didn't reach for his hand. Didn't offer a verse or a phrase designed to make the moment easier. She just stayed in it with him.

"I feel stupid," Marcus said.

"You're not stupid."

"I told them she changed."

"You told them the truth," Megan said. "She did change. For a while."

Marcus shook his head. "Then what was the point?"

Megan set her glass down carefully.

"Marcus, people who are sick don't get better because someone loves them hard enough," she said. "They get better when something inside them finally holds. And that has nothing to do with you."

Marcus stared at the table.

"I know that's not what you want to hear," she added quietly. "But it's the thing nobody told me for a long time about people I loved, and I wish they had."

Marcus's jaw tightened. His eyes were wet now. He pressed his palms flat on the table like he was trying to hold himself in place.

"I can't keep doing this," he whispered.

"You don't have to do it alone," Megan said.

From the other room, Dylan's voice carried softly.

"Marcus?"

Marcus wiped his face with the back of his hand, fast, almost angry about it. He straightened in the chair. The shift happened in less than a second, the broken kid folding himself back into the older brother, the one who made the sandwiches and checked the locks and wrote the D on the paper towel so the lunches didn't get mixed up.

"Yeah," Marcus called back. His voice was steady again. Practiced.

"I gotta go to school tomorrow, right?"

"Yeah. I'll get you up."

Megan watched it happen. The way his whole body reorganized itself around someone else's need. She had seen a lot of kids sit at this table, but she had never seen one disappear that fast into responsibility.

Marcus looked back at her.

"Thank you for dinner," he said.

Megan nodded. "You're welcome here whenever you need to be."

Marcus stood up, pushed the chair in, and walked to the living room to check on his brother.

Megan sat at the table alone for a while after that. She didn't clean the plate. Didn't move the glass. She just sat there thinking about all the ways a kid could grow up too fast and never have anyone notice because he made it look so steady from the outside.

When Jack got home an hour later, the house was dark. Megan was sitting on the porch.

"Marcus was here," she said.

Jack sat down beside her.

"He's not okay, Jack."

Jack nodded. "I know."

"No," Megan said. "I mean he's not okay in a way that football can't fix. He's angry. And he should be."

Jack didn't say anything.

"He told that room about his mother because he believed the story had an ending," Megan said. "And now it doesn't. That's going to cost him something."

They sat there in the dark for a long time.

• • •

Marcus showed up the next morning. Eyes tired. Shoulders tight. Jaw set in a way that dared anyone to ask him how he was doing.

Jack found him near the edge of the parking lot, hands in his pockets, staring at nothing in particular.

"You okay?" Jack asked.

Marcus nodded. "I'm good."

His voice cracked on the word *good*, just enough to betray the automatic lie.

Jack didn't call him on it.

He just nodded once and stood there with him for a moment, both of them looking at the same patch of gravel.

That afternoon, Jack kept practice light. Walk-throughs. No contact. The kind of day that gave everyone room to breathe without admitting they needed it.

Marcus ran his routes without expression. Caught the ball. Jogged back. Didn't talk between reps. Didn't stay after.

• • •

The next day was different.

Marcus came in early. Changed fast. Hit the field before stretching started and ran routes alone on the far side, cutting hard enough that his cleats tore the turf on every break.

Evans noticed first.

"He's running hot," Evans said quietly to Jack.

Jack watched Marcus plant and drive through a route so hard he nearly lost his footing. "Yeah."

"You want me to—"

"Not yet."

Practice moved into team periods. Inside run drill. Tyler and Marcus lined up on the same side. Tyler was doing his job, the same way Tyler always did his job, with his pads low and his motor running and no concern for anyone's feelings on the other side of the ball.

The play called for Marcus to crack down on the linebacker. Tyler filled the hole and met him at the point of attack. Clean hit. Hard, but clean. Tyler drove through the contact the way he'd been taught, finished the play, and started walking back to the huddle.

Marcus didn't get up right away.

When he did, he came up fast.

He shoved Tyler in the back with both hands. Tyler stumbled forward two steps, turned around, and his eyes went flat immediately. Tyler didn't back up. Didn't yell. He squared his shoulders and stepped forward because that was what Tyler did when someone put hands on him.

"Hey!" Evans blew the whistle hard.

Cole got there first. He stepped between them and put one hand on Marcus's chest. Didn't push. Didn't pull. Just planted himself there like a wall that wasn't moving.

"Stop," Cole said. Quiet. Not a request.

Marcus's chest heaved under Cole's hand. His eyes were locked on Tyler.

Tyler stared back. Not angry. Confused. He hadn't done anything wrong and he knew it.

Evans grabbed Marcus by the back of the shoulder pads and pulled him off the field. The rest of the team stood frozen in the drill, helmets turning, nobody sure what had just happened.

"Reset!" Jack called from across the field. "Run it again."

Practice continued.

Evans walked Marcus to the bleachers. Marcus ripped his helmet off and sat down hard, elbows on his knees, hands gripping the back of his neck.

Evans sat beside him.

Neither spoke for a full minute.

"I'm fine," Marcus said.

"I didn't ask."

Marcus's jaw worked back and forth. His breathing was still ragged.

"He didn't do anything to me," Marcus finally said. "Tyler didn't do anything."

"I know," Evans said.

"I just…" Marcus's voice thinned. He pressed his fists against his temples. "I don't know what to do with it. It just sits there."

Evans nodded slowly.

"When I was about your age," Evans said, "my old man lost his job and took it out on everything in the house that couldn't hit back. I spent about six months wanting to fight every person who looked at me wrong."

Marcus glanced at him.

"Didn't have anything to do with them," Evans said. "Had everything to do with the fact that the thing I was actually mad at was something I couldn't swing on."

Marcus stared at the field. The drill was running again. Tyler was back in it, same motor, same effort, like nothing had happened.

"You're not in trouble," Evans said. "But you owe Tyler."

Marcus nodded.

"And you need to eat something. When's the last time you ate a real meal?"

Marcus didn't answer, which was answer enough.

Evans stood up. "Come on. We're going to the field house. I've got granola bars in my office that taste like cardboard, but they'll hold you."

Marcus almost smiled. Almost.

He followed Evans off the bleachers.

• • •

After practice, Tyler found Marcus near the parking lot.

Marcus tensed when he saw him coming.

Tyler stopped a few feet away. He had his bag over one shoulder and his keys in his hand.

"You need a ride?" Tyler asked.

Marcus blinked. "What?"

"A ride. You need one?"

Marcus looked at him for a long moment, waiting for the rest of it, the lecture, the confrontation, the part where Tyler told him what he thought about getting shoved from behind.

It didn't come.

"I'm good," Marcus said quietly.

Tyler nodded once and walked to his truck.

Marcus stood there after he left, watching the taillights pull out of the lot, and felt something shift in his chest that he didn't have a name for yet.

• • •

That night, Jack sat at the kitchen table. Megan poured coffee and sat across from him.

"Marcus went after Tyler at practice," Jack said.

Megan's eyes narrowed slightly. "What happened?"

"Clean drill. Tyler finished a rep. Marcus shoved him from behind. Cole and Evans broke it up."

Megan held her mug with both hands. "And Tyler?"

"Asked Marcus if he needed a ride home after practice."

Megan nodded slowly, like that told her everything she needed to know about the kind of kids in that locker room.

"You can't save them," she said gently.

Jack nodded. "I know."

"But you can stay," she added.

Jack thought about Neil walking back into the locker room on Tuesday.

About Marcus showing up even when his world was slipping again.

About Cole stepping between two teammates without hesitating.

About Tyler offering a ride to the kid who'd just hit him from behind.

Maybe this was the answer. Not fixing. Not rescuing. Just staying.

CHAPTER TWENTY-THREE

Momentum Isn't Loud—It's Earned

Momentum didn't arrive with fireworks.

It showed up quietly, the way habits always do, one practice at a time, one rep stacked on another until nobody could remember where the turning point actually was, only that something had begun to feel steadier than it used to.

The week after Neil's return felt fragile.

Not broken.

Fragile in the way a structure feels when it's finally standing on its own, stronger than before, but still settling, still learning how to carry weight.

Jack knew the difference now.

Due to the funeral, the next Team Theme went up without ceremony on Wednesday.

ACCOUNTABILITY

Jack stepped back and let the seniors speak.

Tyler stood in front of the room, helmet tucked under his arm, shifting his weight once before he started.

"Accountability isn't Coach yelling," Tyler said. "It's us not letting each other slide."

He looked around the room, not rushing, letting the words land.

"If you miss something, own it. If I miss something, you tell me. That's how this works now."

Heads nodded, not dramatic, not loud. Just understanding.

Marcus sat forward, elbows on his knees. Neil listened quietly. Cole watched Tyler like he was storing something away for later, the way quarterbacks do when they recognize leadership forming in real time.

Practice got harder, not louder, not longer, just harder in the way that matters: sharper angles, quicker reads, no tolerance for the small surrenders that used to pass unnoticed.

Mistakes were corrected immediately by teammates.
Missed assignments were owned.
Late arrivals were handled without drama.

No speeches were needed.

The work itself was starting to speak.

• • •

In the locker room afterward, someone waited for the speech about records. About standings. About how close they were getting.

It never came.

Jack talked about footwork. About pad level. About one missed assignment they'd fix on Monday.

The assistants noticed first.

"He won't say the word," Coach Evans muttered as they walked out.

Another coach nodded. "He hasn't in weeks."

Winning used to be the headline.

Now it was barely mentioned.

And Jack knew that was the point.

• • •

Neil seemed to be finally ready for Friday.

Didn't start.
Didn't complain.

He played special teams. Ran down on kickoff like it mattered.

The stands were fuller than they had been a few weeks earlier.

Fuller in a way that felt different, people leaning forward, conversations quieter, attention sharper. Word had spread. Iron Valley was playing for something now.

And everyone knew what one more win would mean.

Springdale struck first. A missed fit turned into a long run, and suddenly Iron Valley was down early.

Two years ago, that would have been enough to unravel them.

Now nobody panicked.

On the next drive, a false start pushed Iron Valley behind the chains. The old version of this team would have tightened up, forced something, tried to fix everything in one play.

Tyler stepped into the huddle before the coaches could say a word.

"Reset," he said quietly. "Next play."

No frustration.
No pointing.

Just reset.

Cole nodded. The offense lined up again.

Iron Valley fell behind early.

Didn't flinch.

Cole managed the game instead of trying to carry it. Marcus blocked on the perimeter without being asked, sealing the edge on a run that steadied the drive and steadied the sideline with it.

Late in the third quarter, Neil rotated in on defense.

Springdale faced 2nd and 5 near midfield.

The ball was snapped.

Inside zone.

Neil read it clean, the guard stepping down, the back pressing the gap just long enough to sell it. Neil stepped downhill and met the runner square, shoulder to chest, the collision echoing in the cool air. The runner churned, twisting, trying to fall forward, but Neil held on, driving his feet until help arrived and the whistle cut through the noise.

They both went down hard.

Neil lay there a second longer than usual, staring up at the lights, breath coming fast, chest rising and falling as the noise of the stadium washed over him.

Then he rolled to a knee, stood, and jogged back to the huddle like it was just another rep.

Tyler slapped his helmet as he passed.

"Good fit."

Neil nodded once.

That was enough.

• • •

The game stayed tight into the fourth quarter.

Iron Valley needed one drive, not a miracle, not a big play, just a drive built on patience and trust.

Cole led the way.

Short throws.
Inside runs.
Clock moving.

The kind of drive that required discipline more than talent.

Third down near the red zone.

Cole dropped back. Pressure pushed the pocket inward, feet closing around him, noise rising.

For a moment, everything slowed.

He stepped up, found space, and fired over the middle.

Marcus caught it in stride.

A defender hit him at the five. Marcus staggered, nearly went down, then spun through the contact and fell across the goal line.

Touchdown.

The sideline erupted. Loud enough to release the tension that had been building all night.

Marcus jogged toward the sideline, breathing hard, adrenaline still surging through him.

As he reached the boundary, he glanced into the stands.

He saw his younger brother Dylan.

Standing against the railing, both hands gripping it, eyes wide, grinning like he'd just seen something impossible.

Marcus slowed for just a second.

He pointed at him.

Dylan pointed back, bouncing on his toes, laughing.

For a moment, the noise faded.

Marcus blinked hard once, turned, and pulled his helmet back on.

Iron Valley burned the clock on the final possession and finished it.

Jack smiled for exactly one second.

• • •

That night, Megan's house filled again.

Quieter laughter. Longer conversations. Plates emptied. No one asked if it was okay to stay anymore; it had simply become understood that this was where people came now.

Neil sat closer.
Tyler laughed more easily.
Cole leaned against the wall, listening more than talking.

At one point, Cole was telling a story about Jack making him run extra sprints after a bad read in practice.

"My dad thinks if he runs me enough, I'll stop throwing off my back foot," Cole said, shaking his head. "I told him, 'Man, you're not even my position coach.' He just pointed at the line and said, 'Run.'"

Tyler laughed. Marcus grinned.

Neil didn't.

His face didn't change much, just a small flinch around the eyes, the kind most people would miss. But Cole caught it. The laughter drained out of him fast.

"Neil…" Cole started.

Neil shook his head. "It's fine."

"I wasn't thinking," Cole said quietly. "I'm sorry."

Neil looked at him for a second, then nodded once. "Tell the rest of the story. It was funny."

Cole didn't finish the story.

Marcus lingered in the kitchen after most people drifted out.

Megan wrapped leftovers quietly.

"She's in rehab," Marcus said.

Megan nodded gently. "I know."

Marcus stared at the counter for a long time.

"I thought I'd just be mad," he said quietly. "But I'm not just mad."

He swallowed.

"I'm sad too."

The words seemed to surprise him as much as anyone.

"I keep thinking about when things were normal," he said softly. "Before everything got… like this."

Megan rested a hand lightly on his shoulder.

"You don't have to pick which one you feel," she said.

Marcus nodded, eyes fixed on the counter, shoulders finally loosening a little.

"Thanks," he said.

She watched him gather up Dylan and act like nothing was wrong as he took him home.

• • •

By Sunday morning, Iron Valley fans knew they had tied the most wins the program had seen in ten years.

Administration noticed.
Fans noticed.
The town noticed.

More than that, the standings noticed.

One more win would set up something Iron Valley hadn't played for in a long time.

A conference title game.

Even though in this area, there was one game that would mean even more than a conference title.

Jack didn't mention it.

He didn't need to.

• • •

The final Team Theme before Week 9 went up on Monday morning.

Jack stood there longer than usual before writing it.

COMPOSURE

The squeak of the marker seemed louder in the quiet room.

He stepped back and looked at the word for a long moment.

Ten years ago, he would have written WIN in all caps and underlined it twice.

Now the word composure felt heavier. Truer. Harder to achieve and easier to lose.

"This week isn't different because of who we play," he said finally. "It's different because of how loud everything will be."

Phones buzzed. Everyone already knew.

West Ridge.
Undefeated.
Five miles away.

Iron Valley had won enough now that it couldn't be ignored.

But what stood out to the players, to the assistants, even to the parents lingering at practice, was what Jack didn't talk about.

He didn't talk about records.
Didn't talk about standings.
Didn't talk about winning.

He talked about spacing. About eyes. About effort when nobody was watching.

Coach Evans said it out loud one afternoon.

"He's different," he said quietly. "It's not about the scoreboard."

Tyler heard it and nodded.

The kids already knew.

As Jack erased the board late that afternoon, he paused and looked at the word one more time.

COMPOSURE.

Week 9 was here.

And Iron Valley hadn't arrived chasing wins.

They had arrived chasing something harder.

Something that lasted.

CHAPTER TWENTY-FOUR

Hold the Line

By Monday morning, the whole town knew what week it was.

Most years they tried to pretend it wasn't.

West Ridge week was something you downplayed if you were Iron Valley. Something you shrugged off with jokes and routine, because treating it like a big deal only made the loss feel louder. You told yourself it was just another game, and everyone nodded like they believed it.

They did that because they had to.

Because no one talked about the last time Iron Valley beat West Ridge.

Not because they didn't remember.

Because it had never happened.

But this year felt different.

Teachers wore Iron Valley shirts to school. The lunchroom buzzed louder than usual. Someone had already hung a hand-painted banner near the gym entrance—BEAT WEST RIDGE—letters uneven, paint still drying at the edges.

Jack passed two custodians in the hallway, arguing about the score like it had already been played.

"I'm telling you," one of them said, sweeping without looking up, "they got a shot."

The other shook his head. "They got more than a shot."

Jack kept walking.

People believed.

That was the dangerous part.

West Ridge week didn't sneak up on anyone.

Jack looked at the theme one more time before anyone arrived to make sure it fit this week.

It did.

No underline.
No explanation yet.
Just one word.

COMPOSURE

• • •

Jack was walking the sideline before practice when he noticed a familiar stance near the gate—hands in pockets, shoulders slightly forward, watching drills like he'd never stopped.

Ray Holloway.

Ray looked older.

Not weaker.
Just quieter.

Jack slowed.

Ray didn't wave. Didn't smile. He waited.

"Coach," Ray said.

Jack nodded. "Ray."

They stood there a moment, practice noise filling the space.

"Kids look good," Ray said.

"They're working," Jack said.

They watched together for a while. Tyler coaching up a younger lineman on his hand placement. Marcus running a route at three-quarter speed, talking a sophomore through the footwork. Neil walking a younger kid through a coverage read between reps.

"Heard about the Parker kid," Ray said. "His dad."

"Yeah."

"You handled that well." Ray said it flat, one coach to another. No sentiment behind it. Just an observation.

Jack tried to read what was underneath the visit. Couldn't tell if Ray was reaching out or just passing through. Maybe it didn't matter.

"I'm pulling for them," Ray said. "I want you to know that."

He didn't say anything about the season. Didn't say Jack was right. Twenty-two years doesn't dissolve in one season, and Ray wasn't a man who pretended otherwise.

"Appreciate you coming by," Jack said.

Ray gave a short nod. Then he turned, walked back through the gate, and didn't look back.

Jack watched him go. It wasn't an apology. Wasn't a surrender. It was something smaller and harder to name—two men standing on opposite sides of a fracture, both choosing not to make it worse.

It was enough for now.

Jack turned back to practice.

Tyler was already calling out a coverage adjustment before the whistle.
Neil adjusted a freshman's stance without being asked.
Marcus ran an extra rep on his own.

The energy wasn't louder.

It was tighter.

• • •

Wednesday practice started clean.

Neil rotated in with the second-team defense during inside run. The same drill he'd been sharp on all week. Read your key, fit your gap, finish the play.

First rep, he was late. Not by much, half a step, but enough for the back to get through the hole untouched. Neil reset without a word.

Second rep, he misread the pull entirely. Went the wrong direction. The offense gained fifteen yards on a play that should have been stuffed.

Jack saw it happen from across the field. Saw Neil standing in the wrong gap, helmet tilted, staring at the ground like he didn't recognize where he was.

Third rep, the ball was snapped and Neil didn't move.

Not frozen, exactly. Just gone. His eyes were open but pointed somewhere the field couldn't reach.

The whistle blew. Players reset. Neil ripped his helmet off and slammed it against his thigh so hard the sound cracked across the field.

"Come on!" he yelled, but it wasn't at anyone else. He was yelling at himself, and it wasn't about the rep.

Everyone heard it. The field got quiet the way fields do when something breaks that wasn't supposed to.

Neil turned and walked off the field. Not toward the sideline. Toward the locker room. Helmet swinging from one hand, the other balled into a fist at his side.

Jack started to follow, but Evans was already moving.

"I got him," Evans said quietly as he passed Jack.

Jack nodded and turned back to the team. "Reset. Next rep."

Practice kept moving. It had to.

Evans found Neil sitting on the bench in front of his locker, elbows on his knees, staring at the floor. His helmet sat upside down beside him. His hands were shaking.

Evans didn't sit right away. He leaned against the locker across from him, arms folded, and waited.

"I can't even do the one thing I'm supposed to be good at," Neil said, voice tight. "Seeing the field. That's the only thing I have. And I can't even do that right now."

Evans let it sit.

"You sleeping?" Evans asked.

Neil shook his head slowly.

"Eating?"

A long pause. "Not really."

Evans nodded. He didn't say anything about the reps. Didn't say anything about Friday. He just stood there, steady, the way a man does when he knows the kid in front of him doesn't need coaching right now. He needs someone to not leave the room.

After a few minutes, Neil exhaled hard, like he'd been holding it since the snap.

"Some days are just bad days," Evans said. "Doesn't mean you're going backwards. Just means it's still in there."

Neil picked up his helmet. Turned it over in his hands. Ran his thumb along the facemask the way he always did when he was thinking.

"I keep seeing his truck in the parking lot," Neil said quietly. "Every time someone pulls in after practice, I look up. I know it's not him. But I still look."

Evans swallowed hard but didn't look away.

"You don't have to stop looking," Evans said.

Neil put his helmet on. Stood up. Walked back toward the field without another word.

He didn't take another rep that afternoon. But he stood on the sideline the rest of practice, watching, the way he always did. Eyes on the field. Hands still.

That was enough for today.

• • •

West Ridge's social media started early.

A post of their stadium, packed bleachers, smoke rolling across the field, their band lined up perfect.

Caption:
Iron Valley ain't ready for this.

By Monday afternoon, there were photos.

A picture of Jack on the sideline, frozen mid-shout.

Comments underneath:

Not even a .500 coach yet.
He knows what's coming.
This run's about over.

Then a picture of Cole.

Caption:
Daddy can't save you on Friday.

More comments:

Coach's kid is getting all the carries.
Guess it helps when daddy calls the plays.
Watch them fold when it gets real.

Then one of Marcus.

Grainy. Zoomed. Mid-route.

Caption:
You won't make it past the 3rd quarter as soft as you are.

And then the one that spread fastest.

A black graphic. White numbers.

0–28

Under it:
All time. Don't forget it.

The comments rolled in from both sides.

History don't lie.
Same movie every year.
About to be 0-29 against us.

Then replies:

Different team this year.
We'll see Friday.

• • •

Neil saw it first.

He didn't say anything. Just showed Marcus.

Marcus scrolled past the "soft" comment, then stopped on the grainy photo of himself mid-route.

He remembered the play, third down, he'd run the wrong route because he'd guessed instead of trusting the call.

The photo captured the moment he realized it too late.

He closed the app, but the image stayed.

Because by the time Marcus put the phone away, a freshman was already talking near the weight room.

"Y'all see what they said about Cole—"

Tyler's head turned slowly.

The freshman stopped talking.

The room went quiet.

Tyler didn't say anything.

He didn't have to.

• • •

Practice that day felt different.

Pads cracked sharper than usual, the sound carrying across the field and bouncing off the empty bleachers. Cleats tore at the turf. The smell of cut grass and sweat hung in the cool afternoon air, breath starting to show faintly when players exhaled between reps.

Voices stayed lower between drills. Fewer jokes. More nods.

Marcus worked like he was trying to burn something out of himself. Every route finished hard. Every block held a second longer than it needed to. When the whistle blew, he was already turning back toward the huddle.

Neil stayed close to Cole most of the afternoon, helmet tucked under one arm, eyes moving across the defense before each snap. Cole would glance over between reps.

"What do you see?"

Neil answered the same way every time. Calm. Precise. Just enough.

Tyler moved through the drills like another coach on the field. A hand on a shoulder pad here. A quick correction to a stance there. Resetting alignments before the ball was snapped again.

From the numbers, Jack noticed a team that was getting ready for the biggest in recent history and one that could shape the school for years to come.

• • •

Cole didn't show the phone to anyone.

He just sat in the locker room after everyone left, thumb frozen on the screen.

The comments kept refreshing, new ones every few seconds.

He didn't cry. Didn't throw the phone.

He just stared until the screen dimmed, then locked it and shoved it in his bag.

Marcus came back in to grab his cleats and saw him.

"You good?"

Cole shrugged. "Yeah."

Marcus leaned against the locker beside him.

"They're acting like I asked for this," Cole said quietly.

Marcus nodded once. "You didn't."

Silence.

"My brother's asking if you're going to beat them," Marcus said.

Cole let out a breath that was almost a laugh.

"He thinks you're Superman."

Cole shook his head slightly.

“He doesn’t care about the score,” Marcus said quietly. “He just wants to see you stand up to them after they talk like that.”

Cole looked at him.

Marcus shrugged. “Same for me.”

They left together.

• • •

That night at Cole’s house, Dylan and Bennett were in the yard tossing a football under the porch light.

The grass was damp from the evening air. The ball made a soft thud each time it landed in their hands, leather slapping against their palms before spinning back the other direction.

When they saw Marcus walking up the drive, both boys ran toward him, the ball tucked under Bennett’s arm.

Dylan started in.

“Can you believe they said—”

Marcus lifted a hand and shook his head gently.

“Not now.”

The boys looked at each other, then nodded.

A moment later, Bennett flipped the ball back to Dylan.

The ball kept moving across the yard.

• • •

Later, Jack sat at the kitchen counter, staring at his phone.

"They went after Cole," he said quietly.

Megan nodded. "I know."

"That's our kid."

"And he's their teammate," she said calmly.

Jack looked up.

Megan held his eyes.

"You don't get to protect him from every word."

Jack didn't answer.

"But you can show him how to handle it."

Jack exhaled slowly.

Megan reached for his hand.

"They're watching you this week," she said. "Not because you're perfect. Because you're their example."

Jack nodded.

The preparation was done.

The noise kept coming.

COMPOSURE.

Iron Valley was ready.

Not because they were perfect.

But because they knew who they were.

And they weren’t giving that away.

CHAPTER TWENTY-FIVE

Five Miles Feels Like Forever (Part I)

Iron Valley had never seen a crowd like this.

Not for football.

Cars lined the roads a mile out. Lawns along the highway had turned into makeshift parking lots. Pickup beds doubled as bleachers. People stood shoulder to shoulder along the fences, pressed three deep where there was nowhere left to sit.

Ten thousand people.

Some inside the stadium.
Some lining the track.
Some were standing along the sideline itself because there was nowhere else to go.

News vans sat behind the end zone, antennas raised like something historic was about to happen, because for the first time in a long time, it was.

Five miles had never felt this far apart.

West Ridge buses got to the game later than normal.

They preferred to warm up on their own indoor and show up in style.

A police escort met them three blocks out. Lights flashing. Sirens chirping just enough to clear a path. The buses crept through crowds already chanting, phones held high, faces painted black, gold, and Iron Valley blue.

In the other locker room, Iron Valley was silent.

Cole stared straight ahead, earbuds in, hearing everything anyway. Marcus sat with his hood up, jaw set, hands clenched and unclenched like he was working something out of his system. Neil leaned forward in his seat, nervous, but trying to take it all in.

His dad would've been the first one in the parking lot tonight. Neil knew that without thinking about it, the same way he knew the man's work boots would've been dusty and his smile would've been the quiet kind, the one he saved for things that mattered. Neil pressed his palms flat against his thighs and breathed.

Tyler Briggs stood at the front of the lockers when they finally stopped.

"Eyes up," he said calmly. "This is what we worked for."

No one answered.

They didn't need to.

As they stepped onto the field for warm-up, the noise hit them like a wave.

West Ridge's crowd roared. Not cheering, but claiming the field. Their side of the stadium was a wall of black and gold, flags whipping, drums pounding. The smell of smoke and grilled meat hung in the air.

West Ridge players were already on the field.

Loose. Confident. Laughing.

They moved through warmups like they owned the place and were just waiting to lay claim to another win.

Iron Valley had been the punchline.

Tonight, they were the obstacle.

Trash talk started early.

A West Ridge receiver jogged past Iron Valley's sideline, yelling about "fake wins" and "soft schedules." A lineman slapped his chest and screamed toward the crowd, soaking it in.

Marcus heard it.

Neil heard it too.

Neil looked at Marcus, eyes searching.

Marcus shook his head once.

Composure.

Jack stood on the sideline, headset on, hands still.

Act right, he reminded himself.

The officials struggled to clear space. Fans pressed closer. The sideline shrank until Iron Valley's players were nearly standing on the painted white line.

"Coach," an official said, breathless. "We're doing our best."

Jack nodded. "I know."

West Ridge finished warmups last.

They always did.

Instead of jogging to their sideline, they gathered at midfield, right on the Iron Valley logo.

Helmets together. Arms locked. A deliberate pause.

The crowd leaned in.

Then it happened.

"F— Iron Valley!"

The chant exploded outward, swallowed instantly by the roar of the West Ridge crowd. Phones went up. Cheers rained down.

Iron Valley froze.

Just for a second.

Neil's face flushed. His jaw tightened. His fists clenched.

Marcus stared straight ahead, nostrils flaring.

Cole took one step forward before Tyler's arm shot out, not grabbing, just touching.

"Don't," Tyler said quietly.

Jack felt it then, the pull. The moment that decided everything.

He turned to the team.

No yelling.

No speech.

"Eyes on me," he said.

They gathered in tight.

"That's not about us," Jack said calmly. "That's about who they are."

He pointed back toward the sideline.

"We don't respond to noise," he continued. "We respond to work."

Tyler nodded. Marcus exhaled slowly. Neil swallowed and straightened his shoulders.

The captains walked out for the coin toss under a wall of sound.

Ten thousand people watched.

Five miles worth of history pressed in from every direction.

As Iron Valley jogged to the sideline, Jack looked once more at the crowd spilling over the fence, at the chaos pressing against order.

This is where it shows, he thought.

Not the scoreboard.

Not the standings.

Who you are when everything is loud and nothing is fair.

The whistle blew.

Iron Valley was ready to find out.

CHAPTER TWENTY-SIX

Five Miles Feels Like Forever (Part II)

Cole jogged past Jack as the teams came out of the locker room, helmet tucked under his arm, face calm in a way that made Jack proud—and uneasy—all at once.

Marcus followed close behind.

No smile.
No glare.

Just focus.

Inside every locker, the same word was taped in block letters.

COMPOSURE

Kickoff.

West Ridge received.

They wasted no time.

Six plays. Seventy yards. Iron Valley missed a tackle it hadn't missed in weeks. The crowd roared, not Iron Valley's roar. West Ridge's. The kind that assumed the ending was already written.

Seven minutes later, West Ridge punched it in.

7–0.

Jack didn't flinch.

But he felt it.

Iron Valley's first drive stalled. A dropped pass. A false start. Punt.

Jack was halfway down the sideline when he heard it.

Cole spoke quickly to Marcus – "They keep taunting me. I can barely hear my own voice over the crowd and them."

Then the correction. Not from a coach.

From Tyler.

"Hey," Tyler said, clapping his hands once. "Just keep your composure."

He looked at Marcus. Then Cole. Then Neil.

"Find a way."

Jack stopped walking.

Didn't turn around.

Didn't say anything.

He didn't need to.

West Ridge came back with rhythm now. Confident. Sharp. Their quarterback moved the chains like he'd done it a hundred times before, because he had.

The ball crossed midfield again.

The noise swelled. Cameras zoomed. Everyone seemed to hold their breath.

Jack felt the weight press in from everywhere—the stands, the cameras, the years.

This is where it used to break, he thought.

Third and long.

West Ridge took a shot.

The quarterback held the ball just a fraction too long.

Marcus saw it.

He didn't hesitate.

He undercut the route and exploded through the receiver—shoulder into chest, helmet clean. The ball tipped up in the air.

Marcus hit the ground hard, rolled once, and came up with the ball.

The Iron Valley sideline erupted.

Marcus didn't celebrate.

He handed the ball to the official and jogged back to the huddle.

Jack exhaled.

Iron Valley capitalized.

Cole ran angry now, but not recklessly. Purposeful.

Four yards. Six. Eight.

He hit the hole low, shoulders square, legs churning through first contact. A linebacker met him in the gap and wrapped him high, but Cole kept driving, twisting sideways and falling forward as two more defenders piled on.

The whistle came late.

As players untangled, a West Ridge defender leaned down near Cole's facemask.

"Daddy ain't out here to protect you." He stared at Cole as he said it.

Cole didn't react.

He stood, handed the ball to the official, and jogged back to the huddle, breathing hard but steady, eyes fixed ahead.

The line fired off together. Tyler sealed the edge, feet driving, hands locked inside, turning the defensive end just enough to open a crease.

Cole burst through it for six more yards before being dragged down from behind.

The sideline came alive. Helmets lifted. Coaches leaning forward. Players stepping closer to the numbers without realizing it.

Second and short.

Cole again.

This time, they met him in the backfield. Three defenders closed at once, arms wrapping, legs driving. For a second, the pile didn't move.

Then Cole's legs started churning.

The pile shifted.

One yard.

Then two.

Then three before the whistle blew.

The huddle formed quickly. No speeches. Just breathing. Just nodding.

Third down.

Marcus split wide.

The snap came.

Marcus drove off the line and cut inside on a slant. The ball hit his hands just as the linebacker arrived, the collision snapping his shoulders back and driving him hard to the turf.

The sound carried across the field.

Marcus held on.

For a moment, he stayed down, the air knocked halfway out of him, the noise of the stadium rushing in and out like waves.

He rolled to his knees and pushed himself up slowly, the ball still tucked tight against his ribs.

As he stood, a defensive back stepped in close, helmet nearly touching his.

"You gonna quit again?" he said quietly.

Marcus didn't answer.

And the drive kept going.

They crossed midfield.

Every yard felt heavier than the last. Jerseys dark with sweat. Hands on hips between plays. Helmets tilting slightly lower.

Cole took another handoff and was hit hard at the line, driven backward before he twisted free and fell sideways for two yards. When he stood, he flexed his fingers once, shaking feeling back into them.

Jack watched from the sideline, jaw tight.

Forty was coming.

Maybe more.

Second down.

A quick hitch to the boundary picked up four yards. Not clean. Not easy. But enough to keep moving.

Third down.

Cole kept it on a draw, lowering his shoulder into the hole, fighting through contact and falling forward for three more yards.

Fourth and short.

The chains stood a few feet away.

The stadium noise changed, not louder, but sharper, like everyone was holding the same breath.

The offense jogged to the line.

Cole stood behind center, hands on his thighs for a moment, catching one breath, then another. He looked left.

Marcus stood wide, hands on his knees, still breathing hard from the slant, still feeling the echo of that hit in his ribs.

Cole straightened and clapped for the snap.

The line fired off low.

Cole took one step forward like he was running inside zone again. The linebackers stepped downhill, bodies collapsing toward the middle.

Then Cole pulled up and flipped the ball outside.

Marcus caught it clean.

For a split second, no one touched him.

Then the corner came flying downhill.

Marcus lowered his shoulder and drove through contact, stumbling across the goal line as the defender wrapped him up and carried him to the turf.

The official's arms went up.

Touchdown.

For a moment, Iron Valley just stood there, like they weren't sure it counted.

The stands shook.

Then the sideline erupted. Helmets slapped. Players shouting. Linemen jogging into the end zone to pull Marcus to his feet.

Cole reached him first, grabbing the front of his shoulder pads and pulling him up.

Marcus was breathing hard, eyes wide, still catching up to what had just happened.

The extra point split the uprights.

7–7.

• • •

West Ridge answered.

Of course they did.

They didn't panic. They didn't rush. They drove methodically and finished with a fade in the corner of the end zone.

14–7.

Jack stared out at the field.

Stay with it.

West Ridge wasn't satisfied with 14–7.

• • •

After another three-and-out, they sped up, trying to end the half the way they always did.

They went too fast.

Turnover.

Iron Valley got the ball back with just under two minutes before halftime.

Last season, Jack would've slowed it down. Taken the air out. Gone to the locker room down seven and called it progress.

He didn't.

Cole took the snap.

Marcus beat press coverage clean on second down. Fifteen yards. Chains moved.

Neil was on the sideline, helmet on, bouncing lightly on his toes, watching every second like he was memorizing it.

Cole scrambled on third down and slid just past the marker.

With thirty seconds left, Iron Valley was inside the red zone.

Cole kept it on a zone read and dove across the goal line.

14–14.

The roar was deafening now.

• • •

West Ridge hurried.

This was where Jack noticed it, the subtle shift. They could've taken the tie and gone in. But it wasn't enough. They wanted control back. Wanted momentum. Wanted to remind everyone who they were.

That decision mattered.

They rushed their personnel. Burned time poorly. Let the clock drip while still trying to be aggressive.

On Iron Valley's sideline, Coach Evans leaned toward Jack.

"They could just take a knee and take this to the half," he said.

When they ran another play with ten seconds left, Jack burned his last timeout.

Behind them, Special Teams Coach Harris was already scribbling on his card.

"They're stepping heavy left," Harris said quickly. "Shield's late. We can get there."

Jack didn't hesitate.

"Attack it," he said.

West Ridge lined up to punt with seconds left.

Harris grabbed the punt block unit.

"Inside gap," he said calmly. "No hero stuff. Hands up. Through the shield."

Neil listened closely.

This was his unit.

The snap came.

A fraction low.

The protection slid late.

Iron Valley punched through.

The ball ricocheted sideways.

Neil saw it.

He didn't think.

He scooped it clean and ran like someone who had learned, too early, how fast everything could disappear.

No one caught him.

Touchdown.

21–14.

The horn sounded as the stadium exploded.

Ten thousand people stood frozen in disbelief before the noise caught up to them.

Neil stood in the end zone, hands on his knees, chest heaving, eyes wet.

Jack watched from the sideline, frozen.

This is why you stay, he thought.

Players poured off the field. Fans screamed. Cameras flashed. West Ridge walked faster than they had all night as they left the field.

• • •

At halftime, the shock was complete.

The crowd buzzed, not sure what it had just witnessed. West Ridge fans quiet. Iron Valley fans almost afraid to believe it.

In the locker room, Jack said nothing.

He didn't need to. They all felt it.

But as Jack looked around at Cole, calm and steady, at Marcus locked in, at Tyler leading the room, at Neil sitting quietly with his helmet at his feet, he knew something else too.

Games like this didn't end at halftime. They revealed who you really were.

CHAPTER TWENTY-SEVEN

Five Miles Comes Up Short

Halftime didn't feel like relief.

It felt like standing on a ledge.

The locker room buzzed—controlled, but alive. Helmets rested on knees. Shoulder pads stayed strapped. Nobody sprawled out. Nobody joked. Sweat dried slowly while eyes stayed locked in.

Tyler Briggs stood near the middle of the room, arms crossed, saying nothing. He didn't need to. The linemen clustered closer to him without realizing it, like gravity had shifted.

Neil sat on the edge of a bench, helmet between his feet, breathing steady. He hadn't played much in the first half, but he'd made the play of the game to that point.

Jack waited for the noise to reach its ceiling.

"Look at me," he said.

They did.

"This game isn't about who wants it more," Jack said calmly. "They want it, and we want it. We know that."

He paused, eyes moving from face to face.

"It's about who can continue to stay in it when it gets hard."

No yelling.
No halftime speech meant for cameras.

West Ridge came out angry.

They always did.

They adjusted fast—shorter routes, quicker tempo, no wasted motion. Iron Valley bent. Then bent again. One missed tackle—one they hadn't missed all night.

Touchdown.

21–21.

The noise shifted. Not louder. Sharper. Uneasy.

• • •

Iron Valley's next possession stalled. West Ridge's defense swarmed now, feeding off the moment. The third quarter drained away in collisions and heavy breaths.

Jack paced less than he used to. He watched more. Trusted more.

This is where it's decided, he thought.
Not by a play. By discipline.

Fourth quarter.

Tie game.

Pressure mounting.

West Ridge drove again. Deep. Third and goal. Their quarterback tried to force a throw into the flat.

Marcus saw it before it happened.

He didn't jump the route.

He waited.

Then he jumped and knocked it down.

Fourth down.

The field goal unit came on.

Pressure up the middle.

Missed.

• • •

Pressure was getting to each side, but Iron Valley was handling it better.

Tyler slapped the nearest lineman's shoulder pads. "Time to go," he said.

Iron Valley took over at their own twenty.

Jack glanced at Cole.

Cole nodded once.

The drive was slow. Methodical. Almost boring—and perfect. Four yards. Five yards. Six. Tyler finished every block. Neil stood on the sideline beside Jack, eyes locked on the field, whispering reminders he didn't even realize he was saying out loud.

Midway through the fourth, Jack called it.

Play-action. Same look they'd shown all night.

Cole dropped back, eyes right.

Marcus slipped inside the safety.

For a split second, everything went quiet.

The ball hit Marcus in stride.

He braced for contact—and ran through it.

Touchdown.

28–21.

The crowd exploded.

Jack clenched his jaw.

Not yet.

Neil sprinted onto the field with the extra point team. Celebrating like he didn't have a care in the world.

• • •

West Ridge pushed again. Faster now. Riskier. Their quarterback forced a throw across the middle.

Another turnover.

Iron Valley couldn't move the ball.

But they did bleed the clock. Made every second hurt.

Punted back to West Ridge.

With under four minutes left, West Ridge went for it on fourth down.

Another pick.

Turnover number six.

Jack looked at the field, then at the clock.

"Finish it," he said.

• • •

Iron Valley finished it.

35–21.

The horn sounded, but you couldn't hear it.

People poured over the rails. Onto the track. Onto the field. Parents. Students. Alumni. Faces Jack didn't recognize and faces he'd never forget.

Tyler dropped to one knee near midfield, head bowed, hands on his thighs. A lineman wrapped him up from behind. Then another.

Marcus stood frozen for a moment, helmet off, hands on his head, eyes wide, searching for something that finally felt real.

Cole found him and pulled him in tight.

Neil stood nearby as the trophy was carried toward midfield, tears streaking down his face. He wiped them away with the heel of his hand and laughed through it.

Jack didn't move right away.

He let it wash over him: the lights, the noise, the cameras, the disbelief.

Five miles.

That was all it ever was.

The trophy felt heavier than it looked when they handed it to him, not because of metal or tradition, but because of the hands that had earned it.

Tyler touched it first. Then Marcus. Then Neil. Then Cole.

Pictures flashed. Arms raised. Fireworks lit up the air.

But the celebration didn't end there.

It spilled into the locker room.
Into the parking lot.
Into kitchens and living rooms and driveways across Iron Valley.

The trophy sat in the middle of Megan's kitchen long after midnight, passed from hand to hand. Players came and went. Marcus and Dylan stayed all night. Parents hugged kids they'd watched lose for years. Tyler sat at the table telling the same story over and over, smiling every time like it was the first.

Neil fell asleep on the couch, still in team gear, trophy leaning against the coffee table within arm's reach.

Marcus stood on the back porch at one point, phone pressed to his ear, voice low.

"She saw it," he said quietly. "On TV."

Cole stood beside him, saying nothing. Just there.

As the house finally quieted and the night began to thin, Jack stared at the trophy one last time.

This time, he smiled.

Not because they won.

But because they had become something worth winning.

Five miles up the road, Iron Valley finally mattered.

CHAPTER TWENTY-EIGHT

Empty Banner

Winning the rivalry didn't end the season.

It changed it.

The week after West Ridge felt strange, lighter, louder, dangerous in a way Jack didn't trust. Hallways buzzed. Phones kept lighting up. Strangers stopped him in the grocery store and said his name as they'd always known it.

Jack kept reminding himself, and the team, how fragile momentum could be.

• • •

On Monday night, the school held a pep rally.

The gym filled early, students, teachers, parents lining the walls. The band played louder than usual, the sound echoing off the rafters. Old banners hung from the ceiling, faded years and distant memories watching from above.

Jack stood near the back with the assistants, arms folded, watching.

The players sat together on the floor. Jerseys on. Some smiling. Some uncomfortable with the attention. Tyler sat upright, eyes forward. Marcus leaned back on his hands, scanning the crowd. Neil sat near the end of the row, taking it all in quietly.

When the principal handed Jack the microphone, the gym settled.

He didn't speak long.

"We're proud of these kids," Jack said. "But Friday still matters. So we'll go back to work tomorrow."

A few students laughed softly.

The band started again. The noise returned.

But Jack noticed something as the players stood to leave.

They weren't acting like a team satisfied.

They were acting like a team preparing.

• • •

The next morning, Jack wrote the Team Theme on the board.

STEADY

Under it, one sentence:

Be the same team on Friday that you are on Tuesday.

He didn't explain it.

He didn't need to.

• • •

Practice that week was intentionally boring.

Inside run.
Footwork.
Indy periods stretched longer than usual.

No speeches about rankings.
No talk about playoffs.

Just details.

Tyler Briggs noticed immediately.

When energy drifted, Tyler pulled it back. When laughter got loose, he settled it without raising his voice.

"This isn't over," he said more than once. Not loud. Just certain.

The younger players listened to him now. Not because he demanded it, but because they trusted him.

Neil stayed close to Tyler all week, asking questions, listening more than he spoke. He still wasn't a starter, but he was part of everything now. Belonged in a way he hadn't earlier in the year.

Jack saw it in small ways.

Neil stepping into drills without hesitation.
Players looking to him on special teams.
A helmet tap from Marcus after a rep.

Belonging didn't arrive loudly.

It settled in quietly.

• • •

The final regular-season game decided the conference.

Iron Valley had never won one.

Even in the year they won a state title decades ago, they hadn't taken the conference. The banner space above the gym doors had always stayed empty—like the school didn't quite believe it would ever need filling.

• • •

Friday night came cold and clear.

Warmups stretched across the field. Lines of players moving in rhythm. Balls snapping through the air. Cleats biting into turf.

Neil jogged toward the sideline to grab water and glanced into the stands without really thinking about it.

Then he saw her.

His mom stood near the front row, bundled against the cold, wearing an Iron Valley hoodie that looked brand new and a knit cap pulled low. She waved when their eyes met, not dramatic, just proud.

Neil lifted a hand back, shoulders settling, something inside him easing.

Marcus followed his eyes.

"Your mom?" he asked.

Neil nodded.

Marcus smiled slightly. "That's good."

Neil turned back toward the field.

• • •

Near the fence, Bennett sat beside Dylan, both of them bundled in oversized Iron Valley hoodies, faces painted in school colors. Dylan gripped the rail, talking fast, explaining something about last week's game like he was already breaking down film.

Megan stood just behind them, smiling, hands tucked in her jacket pockets.

Jack saw them as he walked the sideline.

Bennett caught his eye and gave him a thumbs-up.

Jack returned it.

Then he went back to pre-game warmups.

• • •

The opponent came in desperate and physical.

They tried to speed Iron Valley up. Tried to bait them into mistakes. Tried to make the night emotional instead of precise.

Iron Valley didn't bite.

The game wasn't flashy. It wasn't dramatic. It was disciplined football.

Tyler anchored the line, calling out adjustments before coaches could. Cole took what was there. Marcus caught passes that mattered and blocked just as hard when the ball went the other way.

Neil played special teams early, then rotated in late on defense, filling gaps, doing things that didn't show up in headlines but mattered to people who understood football.

On one series, Marcus finished a block near the sideline and jogged back toward the huddle.

As he turned, he heard a small voice from the stands.

"Marcus!"

He glanced up.

Dylan stood gripping the rail, shouting like the game depended on it. Bennett yelled beside him, just as loud.

Marcus lifted a hand briefly.

The next rep, he drove his block longer than he needed to, finishing through the whistle, feet churning until the defender stumbled backward.

Tyler slapped his helmet.

"That's it."

Marcus didn't answer.

But he was breathing harder now.

• • •

Late in the game, when they needed it, they kept it simple.

Third and six.

The noise rolled down from the stands in waves. Two seasons ago, that sound would have sped them up.

Cole stepped to the line, looked once to the sideline, then back to the defense.

"Trips right. Stick," he said quietly.

The snap came clean. Marcus settled in the window and turned upfield the moment the ball hit his chest.

Seven yards. First down.

No celebration.

Just the chains moving.

• • •

When the horn sounded, Jack didn't look at the scoreboard.

He looked at the seniors.

Some cried openly. Others stared at the field like they were afraid it might disappear if they blinked.

Conference champions.

The words didn't feel real at first.

Tyler hugged Jack first.

"Thank you, Coach."

Jack nodded, not trusting himself to say much.

Then the noise began to build.

Students gathered near the fence again. Parents drifted down from the stands. The band kept playing.

A few minutes later, the athletic director walked across the field carrying a small trophy.

He motioned for Jack and the captains.

The team gathered near midfield.

"This school has had great teams," the AD said. "Great players. Even a state championship."

He paused.

"But we have never won a conference championship."

The words settled over the field.

"Until tonight."

Applause rolled across the stadium.

The AD handed the trophy to Jack.

Jack held it for only a second.

Then he turned and handed it straight to Tyler.

"This is yours."

Tyler looked stunned for half a heartbeat, then took it, and the seniors crowded in around him.

The players erupted, not wild, but loud and full, and real emotion pouring out of them.

Pictures followed.

Parents on the field. Phones flashing. Players laughing. Neil stood with his mom for a picture, both of them smiling in a way that didn't need words. Marcus crouched beside Dylan and Bennett, letting them touch the trophy for a second.

For a while, no one wanted to leave.

Players walked the field slowly, still in pads, talking, laughing, replaying moments like they were trying to memorize them.

• • •

Jack found Megan near the fence.

For a moment, neither of them said anything.

Then he pulled her into a hug.

She held on a second longer than usual.

"I'm proud of you," she said softly.

Jack shook his head. "I'm proud of them."

She smiled. "I know."

Nearby, Bennett and Dylan were still talking about the game like it had just started.

Jack watched them for a moment, then turned back toward the field.

• • •

Later, after the field had mostly cleared, Jack stood near the gym entrance alone.

Above the doors, the banner space was still empty.

For years, it had stood there, blank, waiting, almost impossible to imagine filled.

Tonight it looked different.

Not full yet.
But ready.

Jack looked up at it for a long time.

He thought about the August mornings when no one believed.
The October nights when no one spoke.
The empty locker that still sat in his head sometimes.

And now this.

He exhaled slowly.

Winning hadn't changed Iron Valley.

What they had become, together, quietly, rep by rep, while they were winning… that was what would stay.

The banner would go up later.

The real change already had.

CHAPTER TWENTY-NINE

Belief

The playoff game felt different from the moment Iron Valley arrived.

People were already there. Not crowds yet, just clusters.

Parents leaned along the fence with hands buried in jacket pockets. Former players stood near the rail nodding to each other like they were recognizing something familiar again. Kids in oversized hoodies tossed footballs in the corner of the end zone like this was just another Friday night, even though everyone knew it wasn't.

The lights came on before warmups finished, glowing against a sky that hadn't fully darkened yet. The band stayed on the fight song longer than usual, repeating it once, then again, like no one wanted the night to move forward too quickly.

Jack walked the sideline during stretch with his hands in his pockets, letting himself feel it.

This wasn't noise.

This was expectation.

Not pressure.

Belief.

Across the field the stands kept filling with teachers, custodians, kids who hadn't been to a game all year, and older men who sat in the same seats every fall no matter how the season went.

A few of those older men now leaned along the rail near midfield. Former players. Some had driven back for the game. They stood with their arms folded watching warmups with quiet intensity.

History didn't shout.

It watched.

Jack looked down the line of players.

No one laughed loudly. No one looked tight either.

Just ready.

Tyler walked past, tapping shoulder pads as he went, saying little but making sure everyone was there. Marcus stood near the numbers, rolling his shoulders loose, eyes fixed on the field. Cole jogged routes with the receivers, breathing steady, focused but calm.

Jack glanced once more at the stands before turning back toward the field.

They belonged here.

The band played louder now, like nobody wanted the night to feel ordinary.

…

Jack had introduced the theme quietly on Monday.

No board.

No long speech.

Just one word spoken aloud.

BELIEF.

"You don't earn this by what you did last week," he told them. "You earn it by being who you are again."

The players nodded.

By that point, they understood.

Belief wasn't about confidence.

It was about trust.

Trusting the work.
Trusting the teammate beside you.
Trusting that the next play still mattered even when the last one didn't go your way.

That had been their season.

Now it was the playoffs.

…

Warmups felt different too.

The other team was bigger. Deeper. More bodies rotating through drills. Longer strides. Sharper cuts. You could see it without trying.

Iron Valley saw it too.

And they kept warming up.

Cole jogged past Jack on his way back from throwing routes, breathing steady and calm. Marcus adjusted his gloves and glanced once toward the stands before turning back to the field. Tyler walked the line tapping shoulder pads as he passed.

No speeches.

No theatrics.

Just readiness.

…

The game started tight.

Playoff football usually did.

Every yard mattered. Every tackle carried a little more weight. The first quarter passed with both teams trading field position while the defenses settled in.

Iron Valley's offense found rhythm midway through the second quarter.

Cole kept the ball twice on reads, sliding forward for extra yards instead of forcing anything. Marcus absorbed contact on third down and held on, the ball thumping against his chest like a second heartbeat as the chains moved. Tyler finished a block that turned two yards into six before jogging calmly back to the huddle.

Twelve plays.

Nothing flashy.

Everything right.

The drive ended in the end zone.

Iron Valley never gave the lead back.

…

The game never felt comfortable.

The opponent stayed close. The crowd stayed loud. Every possession seemed to matter more than the last.

Late in the third quarter, Iron Valley's defense faced a fourth down near midfield.

Neil stepped onto the field.

The snap came clean. The runner cut inside. Neil filled the gap.

The tackle popped loud enough to echo under the lights.

The stadium erupted.

Neil popped up first, chest heaving, then jogged off as Tyler slapped his helmet.

"Atta boy."

Neil nodded once, fighting the grin.

…

The fourth quarter stretched longer than the rest of the game combined.

When the final horn sounded, the scoreboard showed something Iron Valley hadn't seen in more than two decades.

For a moment, the players didn't celebrate.

They just stood there looking at it.

Then the sideline poured onto the field.

Parents climbed the rail. Younger kids ran across the end zone chasing players who had suddenly become heroes for the night. Phones appeared everywhere as families gathered near midfield for pictures.

Marcus stood near the numbers with Dylan and Bennett beside him while someone lined up a picture. Dylan grinned widely and threw an arm around Marcus's waist while Bennett stood on the other side trying to look serious for the camera.

Before the picture finished, Cole jogged over and dropped beside them, laughing.

That opened the floodgates.

Soon, the seniors gathered together. Then the linemen pulled in the receivers. Someone called for the whole team. Helmets were set on the turf while players crowded shoulder to shoulder near midfield.

A parent counted down.

Flash.

The full team picture.

Even Jack got pulled into one.

A mother handed him a phone and waved him into the middle of a group of players and families. Jack shook his head once but stepped in anyway while arms wrapped around shoulders and younger players leaned close.

Another flash.

For a few minutes, the field didn't feel like a football field anymore.

It felt like a town gathering in the middle of the night.

Jack drifted back toward the sideline afterward, watching families linger near the numbers while kids chased each other across the painted yard lines.

Near the rail, one of the former players laughed softly and shook his head.

"Twenty-two years," he said.

The words carried quietly through the group around him.

Twenty-two years.

…

Eventually, the players drifted back toward the locker room with families following them down the walkway.

Inside, the noise continued.

Music blasted from someone's phone. Shoulder pads thumped against lockers. Players shouted across the room while a few younger ones repeated the score like they still didn't believe it.

Marcus jumped onto a bench and slapped the ceiling tile before dropping back down. Tyler sat for a moment, unlacing his cleats, before someone shoved him and pulled him back into the middle of the room. Neil stood near his locker, grinning while two seniors replayed his fourth-down tackle like it had happened five minutes ago.

Jack stood in the doorway for a moment, watching.

Then he stepped inside.

"How about one more week!"

The room exploded.

Helmets lifted. Towels spun. Someone pounded on a locker hard enough to rattle the hinges.

"One more week!" someone yelled back.

Jack laughed and shook his head.

That was enough speech for the night.

…

The town noticed the next morning.

People stopped Jack at the gas station before sunrise. A cashier at the grocery store leaned across the counter just to say congratulations. Teachers mentioned the game between classes while students replayed the fourth-down stop in the hallway like they had been standing on the sideline.

Practice on Monday felt different.

Energy buzzed across the field before drills even started. Players moved faster between stations, and coaches had to pull them back into line more than once just to keep the pace under control.

Jack waited until the stretch ended before walking toward the team.

He shared one word.

ENDURE.

And gave this description.

Stay steady when it gets hard.

Everyone understood what waited in Round Two.

Lake City.

Defending State Champions.

A chance to win the first sectional title Iron Valley had seen since 1980.

Jack capped the marker and stepped back toward the door.

Practice started again.

…

The week moved quickly.

Film sessions ran longer. Walkthroughs stayed sharp. Even the younger players seemed to understand something bigger was coming.

Tyler spent most practices talking to the linemen between reps, correcting small details that usually waited until the sideline. Marcus stayed after drills, running routes until the lights came on. Cole moved carefully through stretches early in the week before loosening up by Thursday.

Nearby, Neil watched the older players prepare and tried to mirror it.

The games were getting bigger.

So were the moments inside them.

…

The bus ride that Friday felt heavier than any ride that season.

Not tense.

Just settled.

The bus hummed steadily as it rolled through the dark, the low vibration of the engine filling the silence. Streetlights slid across the windows, turning helmets into silhouettes for a second at a time.

No one joked.

No one slept.

A few players listened to music but most stared ahead, lost in their own thoughts.

Tyler sat near the front with his forearms resting on his knees, staring straight ahead like the game had already started in his mind.

Two rows back, Neil watched the passing lights instead of his phone, as if he were trying to memorize the ride.

Marcus leaned his forehead against the cold glass.

Cole sat beside him quietly with his ankle wrapped tight.

Jack noticed all of it.

He said nothing.

Outside the window the road stretched into the dark.

Ahead waited the biggest game Iron Valley had played in more than forty years.

And the only word that mattered now was the one written on the board.

ENDURE.

CHAPTER THIRTY

The Section Championship

Round two felt different from the moment Iron Valley arrived.

Lake City was already on the field when the bus pulled in. Bigger bodies. Sharper warmups. Helmets snapped into place with the quiet confidence of a team that had done this before.

Defending State Champions.

The stands filled early. Iron Valley fans packed into their side bundled against the cold while across the field, Lake City's band warmed up with the steady rhythm of a program used to nights like this.

Jack walked the sideline during the stretch with his hands in his pockets, letting himself feel the moment without trying to control it.

He had written one word on the board earlier that week.

ENDURE.

Not flashy football.
Not perfect football.

Just compete and see what happens. The players had nodded. Now it was time to see if they could live it.

They belonged here.

Not because anyone expected them to win.

Because they had earned the chance to try.

…

The locker room was quieter than Jack expected.

Not nervous quiet. Something else.

Players sat at their lockers in different stages of getting ready. Tape pulled tight. Wrists wrapped. Helmets sitting upside down between their feet. The pregame playlist played from someone's speaker near the back wall, but the volume was low, like even the music understood.

Tyler sat at his locker already dressed, pads buckled, wrists taped, staring straight ahead at nothing in particular. His jaw worked slowly on a piece of gum. He looked like a man waiting on something he'd already decided he was ready for.

Marcus sat two lockers down, still as stone, hood up, gloves already on. No bouncing. No nervous energy. He looked the way he always did before big moments now—settled. Like the noise had already come and gone inside his head.

Cole sat on the bench near the training table, ankle wrapped thick, testing the range by rolling it in slow circles. Jack watched him wince once, just barely, then stop testing and pull his sock over it like the conversation was over.

Jack felt the worry rise and let it pass. Cole would play. They both knew that.

Neil sat at the end of the row, helmet in his lap, fingers tracing the facemask the way some people tap a steering wheel when they're thinking. He wasn't starting tonight. He knew that. But his eyes moved around the room like he was memorizing it—every face, every sound, the way the light hit the concrete walls.

Jack stood near the whiteboard where he'd written ENDURE earlier that week. He didn't add anything to it now.

He looked at the room full of kids who had been here before—not in this moment, but in every moment that built toward it. The early morning lifts when nobody believed the season would turn. The film sessions after losses that felt permanent. The nights at his kitchen table when these players were just kids trying to figure out if staying was worth it.

They had answered that question already.

Jack didn't give a speech.

"Let's go to work," he said.

Tyler stood first. Then Marcus. Then the room followed.

They walked out together, cleats clicking against the concrete hallway, echoing off the walls in a rhythm that sounded like something Jack would remember for a long time.

…

Lake City opened with a fourteen-play drive that felt like a slow test of strength. Inside runs that gained four yards at a time. Short passes that pushed the chains. Every tackle finished with two or three defenders leaning forward just to stop the runner's momentum.

Tyler made three tackles on the drive. On the last one, he stepped into the hole and met the back head on, the collision knocking his helmet sideways while his hand bent awkwardly against the runner's shoulder pad.

He stood slowly and flexed his fingers once.

One of them didn't move.

Tyler jogged to the sideline, holding his hand against his chest. The trainer met him halfway.

"Let me see it."

Tyler held the hand out. The finger already angled wrong.

"That's broken," the trainer muttered.

Tyler watched him for a second.

"You can help me or not," he said calmly, "but I'm going back in."

The trainer sighed and guided the finger straight. Tyler didn't flinch. Tape wrapped tightly around the joint, binding the finger to the next one until it couldn't move.

Three plays later, Tyler was back in the huddle.

Lake City finished the drive with a run, off left tackle.

Touchdown.

7–0.

…

Iron Valley answered with a strong opening drive.

Cole kept the ball on a read and slid forward for six. On the next play, Tyler kicked the end inside, and the back burst through the crease for another seven and a first down. The sideline woke up as the offense hurried back to the line.

Cole dropped back and fired a quick out to Marcus near the sideline. Marcus secured the catch and turned upfield for another solid gain.

Behind him, Cole never got up.

A defender had rolled across his ankle as he threw. Cole pushed himself up once, but the leg buckled under him.

The stadium quieted while the trainer jogged out.

Cole finally stood with help, hopping once before putting only the lightest pressure on the ankle as he limped toward the sideline.

Jack glanced at Megan on the sideline, but quickly had to get the backup ready to come in.

Without him, the offense stalled quickly. Two runs disappeared into the line for almost nothing, and the third-down pass sailed wide of Marcus's outstretched hands.

Three plays later, the punt team jogged on.

Jack watched Cole test the ankle on the sideline as soon as he was able.

It didn't look good, but he knew nothing would keep Cole out of this game.

ENDURE.

That was the word.

…

Lake City pushed again, but the defense stiffened near the goal line. Tyler fought through a block and wrapped the runner near the eight. The impact jarred his taped finger, and a sharp pulse shot up his arm, but he reset before anyone noticed.

The field goal made it 10–0.

Cole returned to the field on the next possession with a noticeable limp.

Marcus caught two passes on the drive, and Tyler collapsed the edge on a run that gained seven. The offense began to settle. Short gains. Clean execution. The kind of football that slowed the game down.

On third and goal from the four, Tyler sealed the edge, and Cole slipped through the crease.

Touchdown.

10–7.

They were back in it after being dominated early.

…

Late in the second quarter, the defense forced a punt.

Neil lined up on the edge of the rush unit. The snap came low, and he exploded forward, his hand flashing past the ball as the punter barely got it away.

The kick wobbled sideways.

Iron Valley took over near midfield.

Neil jogged off, trying not to smile while Tyler slapped his helmet as he passed.

"Good rush."

Iron Valley drove again. Marcus caught a crossing route and dragged two defenders forward. Cole rolled right on the next play and found Marcus again near the sideline.

A few plays later, they faced fourth and goal from the three.

Cole looked to the sideline.

Jack nodded.

The ball was snapped.

Marcus caught it at the goal line. The first defender wrapped his legs. The second hit high. Marcus twisted once, drove his knees forward, and fell across the line.

Touchdown.

14–10.

…

Halftime came without celebration.

The locker room door shut behind them, and for a few seconds nobody moved. Just the sound of breathing and pads settling against lockers.

Players sat scattered around the room. Some leaned forward, elbows on knees. Others leaned back with eyes closed, not sleeping, just somewhere else for a moment. The air smelled like sweat and cold grass and the metallic bite of tape adhesive.

Tyler sat in the middle of the room, forearms resting on his thighs, the taped finger stiff inside his glove. He flexed it once, winced, and stopped. Marcus leaned against a locker with his eyes half-closed, breathing slowly, deliberately, like he was rationing something. Cole sat on the bench rubbing his ankle carefully, testing how much weight it could take, his face tight every time it rolled past a certain point.

They were bruised. Tired. Banged up.

But they were here.

Jack stood near the door and watched them. He didn't reach for the whiteboard. Didn't pull out a play sheet. Didn't ask the assistants for adjustments yet.

He just looked at them.

A year ago, a halftime like this would have sent him to the board. Diagrams. Fixes. Adjustments stacked on adjustments, because doing something always felt better than doing nothing. That was the old version of him—the one who believed that if he worked hard enough at the X's and O's, the people part would take care of itself.

He knew better now.

Evans leaned in from the hallway. "You want to go over the adjustments?"

"Give me a minute," Jack said.

He walked to the center of the room and sat down on the bench across from Tyler. Didn't stand over them. Didn't pace. Just sat.

"I'm not going to draw up something new," Jack said. "We don't need new. We need what got us here."

A few eyes opened. A few heads lifted.

"Look around this room," Jack said quietly. "Tyler's got a broken finger and hasn't missed a snap. Cole can barely walk and he scored on one leg. Marcus is making plays all over the field against the defending state champs."

He paused.

"Nobody expected us to be here. Some of you didn't expect it either. That's fine. But you're here. And you're not here because of talent or scheme. You're here because you believe in each other."

The room was still.

"Twenty-four more minutes," Jack said. "That's it. Twenty-four minutes of doing what we've done all year. Nothing fancy. Nothing new."

He looked at Tyler.

"Find a way."

Tyler nodded once, jaw set.

The room held the words for a moment, the way a room does when something true has been said and nobody wants to talk over it.

Then Evans came in with the adjustments. Coaches huddled. Players started retaping, refilling water bottles, pulling helmets back on. The noise returned slowly, purpose replacing silence.

As they filed toward the door, Neil fell into step beside Marcus.

"Twenty-four minutes," Neil said quietly.

Marcus looked at him.

"Twenty-four minutes," Marcus repeated.

They walked out together.

The third quarter crawled by in a grind of punts and field position. Bodies slowed. Everything came harder.

Late in the quarter, Lake City lined up for a field goal and pushed it wide.

The crowd roared like it was a touchdown.

But with ten minutes left, the drive finally came.

Runs that gained four yards at a time, linemen leaning forward into the cold air. Short passes that moved the chains while Tyler fought through blocks, his taped finger throbbing every time his hand caught a jersey.

The touchdown put Lake City back ahead.

17–14.

The teams continued to trade punts after that. Iron Valley's defense barely hung on while the offense struggled to find rhythm.

After another change of possession, the defense held again.

Lake City punted.

The ball bounced once near the fifteen and kept rolling, slow and cruel, until it finally died just outside Iron Valley's goal line.

The official pointed.

One yard line.

Just over three minutes left in the game.

Jack pressed the headset tight against one ear.

"Ball on the one," Coach Evans said. "Let's just get some space here. Run it twice and breathe."

Jack studied the defense crowding the line.

"They're selling out."

"We don't need a disaster here."

Jack looked downfield.

Marcus stood alone with the corner.

The safety cheated inside.

Jack felt the moment.

"Evans."

"Yeah."

"Tell him to take it."

A pause.

"Coach…"

Jack never looked away from the field.

"Let it rip."

Evans exhaled.

"Alright. Let it rip."

Cole glanced to the sideline.

Jack gave the smallest nod.

The snap came clean.

Cole took one step and launched the ball high into the night.

Forty yards downfield, Marcus and the corner rose together. They collided at the forty-five.

Marcus came down with the ball.

The defender fell.

For a second, Marcus just stood there gripping the ball.

Then he saw nothing but green.

He ran.

The sideline exploded. Neil was the first one moving, sprinting down the sideline with the rest of the team pouring behind him.

Thirty.

Twenty.

Ten.

The sound arrived before Marcus crossed the goal line.

Ninety-nine yards later, Iron Valley had the lead.

21–17.

Now, just one stop and they would pull off the upset.

The players could feel the momentum shift.

Lake City had two minutes from their own forty.

Third and twelve.

The receiver dragged his toes along the sideline for the conversion, and the Lake City sideline erupted while Iron Valley slowly reset the defense.

Another set of downs.

Then another third down.

Third and nine.

A dig route across the middle. Marcus stepped into the receiver the moment the ball arrived, the hit cracking across the field.

The receiver held on.

First down.

Iron Valley regrouped near the numbers.

One more stop.

Lake City reached the red zone.

Fourth and goal from the twelve.

The quarterback floated the ball toward the back corner of the end zone.

The wheel route appeared from nowhere.

The receiver caught it.

Touchdown.

24–21.

Forty seconds remained.

Cole completed two quick passes, and the crowd leaned forward with every snap.

As Cole limped forward, the team got set, another quick pass to get out of bounds.

At the 35-yard line with 17 seconds left in the game.

Marcus broke inside on the next play, and Cole stepped into the throw just as the hit arrived.

The linebacker crashed into him.

Cole dropped hard to the turf.

The ball hung too long.

The safety stepped in front.

Interception.

The crowd followed the defender as he fell to the ground with the ball.

Then the play ended.

All eyes turned back.

Cole was still on the turf, breathing hard, one hand gripping the grass as he tried to push himself up. Tyler reached him first while Marcus arrived seconds later.

Cole wiped his eyes.

"I had you," he said as the tears started to come quickly.

Marcus grabbed his arm, and Tyler helped pull him up. Cole tested the ankle once before putting weight on it.

Behind them, Lake City brought the offense onto the field in victory formation.

None of them watched.

The quarterback knelt once.

And the horn sounded.

For a long moment, no one moved.

Not because they were stunned.

Because it was over.

The other team began celebrating at the far end of the field, voices rising, helmets thrown into the night air. The sound carried across the field but felt like it belonged to a different game.

Iron Valley stayed where they were.

Players stood near the sideline staring out at the field like they were trying to hold onto it. Tyler looked once more at the scoreboard, jaw tight, then turned away slowly. Around him, players drifted toward each other. Quiet hugs. Hands on shoulders. Facemasks pressed together longer than usual.

Marcus stood beside one of the linemen, arm across his shoulders, saying nothing. Neil stood a few steps back, helmet still on, breathing hard, eyes shining under the lights.

One younger player sat on the turf staring at the field like someone might tell him there was still time left.

But there wasn't.

Cole found Jack near the thirty-yard line.

He was still limping. His jersey was untucked, grass stains across the numbers, helmet hanging from one hand. His eyes were red and his voice broke before he got the first word out.

"Coach, I'm sorry," Cole said. "I had him. I had Marcus open and I just—"

Jack shook his head.

"Don't."

Cole's chin dropped. His shoulders started shaking, and the tears came harder now, the kind a kid can't stop once they start.

Jack stepped forward and pulled him in.

He held his son for a long time. Not as a coach. Not on the sideline of a football game. Just a father holding his kid on the worst night of his season, letting him know that nothing about this moment changed anything that mattered.

"I'm proud of you," Jack said quietly. "I've never been more proud of you."

Cole gripped the back of Jack's jacket and didn't let go.

Around them, the field slowly emptied. Officials picked up the chains. The scoreboard went dark. The band packed up in sections, instruments disappearing into cases one at a time.

When Cole finally stepped back, he wiped his face with both hands and nodded once, the way he always did when he was putting himself back together.

They walked off the field side by side.

Because that's what they'd always done.

Slowly, the rest of the team followed.

Because the night was finished.

…

The locker room stayed quiet for a long time.

Helmets came off. Shoulder pads unclipped. The seniors gathered in the center of the room with arms around each other.

Tyler stood in the middle of them.

One of the seniors finally said it.

"Coach… we won more games this year than we did our whole career."

The words landed heavier than the loss.

Jack nodded once.

…

…

The season ended without fireworks.

No parade.

No trophy case update yet.

Just change.

…

The next day, Jack stood alone in the locker room.

Tape peeled from the floor. Lockers empty. Silence thick.

He thought about what they'd won.

The conference title.

A playoff game.

But more importantly, a team that believed in themselves.

A team that endured.

Jack turned off the lights and paused at the doorway.

For the first time, the room felt empty.

But not abandoned.

EPILOGUE

What Remains

Five years later, Jack Mercer stood at midfield with his hands in his jacket pockets, the same way he used to on Friday nights.

The lights were on for practice now—not a game—but the place still hummed with energy. Whistles echoed. Pads popped. Voices carried with purpose.

Iron Valley football no longer felt fragile.

Three conference titles hung on the wall now. Clean banners. No dust. No apology. And five miles up the road, West Ridge still circled the date every year.

They hadn't beaten Iron Valley once since that night.

Jack didn't smile at that anymore. Not because it didn't matter, but because it didn't define them.

What defined them was consistency.

He'd learned that the hard way.

That first season had taught him more than the next four combined.
That winning was hard and needed to be earned.
That losing honestly was necessary.
That culture never showed up on a scoreboard first.
And that the most important moments rarely happened under the lights.

Practice broke into team periods. Jack watched the offense jog onto the field, then caught sight of his youngest son, Bennett, slipping into the huddle. Helmet still a little big. Confidence just beginning to settle in. He wasn't the star. Not yet. But he was part of something good, a program that had never known what Iron Valley used to be.

That mattered.

Bennett laughed between reps. Took coaching. Got corrected. Tried again. Jack felt a quiet gratitude for that, for a childhood that included football without carrying the weight of resurrection.

Megan stood near the fence talking with a group of parents, remembering names the way she always had, asking about siblings, school projects, and rides home. New families gravitated toward her without realizing why. She made the place feel smaller and steadier.

On the far sideline, Neil Parker blew a whistle.

Linebackers snapped into position immediately.

Neil looked older now. Stronger. Still quiet. Still deliberate. He'd come back to Iron Valley after his playing days ended. Started as a volunteer. Stayed late. Learned the craft. Earned his spot on the staff.

He didn't need a title to be heard.
The kids followed him anyway.

Grief had never left Neil.

It had just taught him how to stay.

Marcus Reed came back every spring. He said he wanted to see how Dylan was doing, but really, he just wanted to go home.

He stood on the sideline now, broader through the shoulders, calmer in the eyes. College football had given him structure. Discipline. A future that once felt impossible.

Dylan was a freshman now, wearing Marcus's old number. He wasn't the fastest kid on the field or the most talented, but he showed up every day the same way his brother had, early, quiet, ready. He slept in his own bed every night. He ate breakfast at a table. Small things that weren't small at all if you knew where they'd come from.

Marcus watched Dylan run a route during team period and nodded once to himself, the way a man does when something he fought for finally holds.

His mother came by when she could, healthy, present, proud.

She hugged Jack every time she saw him.

"You saved him," she always said.

Jack always shook his head.

"He saved himself."

Cole had gone farther than Jack ever imagined.

College ball. Contributor. Team leader. Film junkie. The kind of player coaches trusted, even when his name wasn't called. He still called Jack after big games, not for praise, but for perspective.

Jack watched him now during a spring visit, clipboard in hand, talking to players like it was the most natural thing in the world.

No longer the coach's kid.

Just a leader.

Tyler was always a leader, and he had not changed since he went to work.

He loved to show up with his wife and little boy to let Coach know he expected him to be an all-state lineman, just like his dad.

Now he was leading a much more important team.

Others came back too, when schedules allowed. Different paths. Different strengths. Same foundation. They'd found their way without needing the game to define them, and Jack counted that as a win he never expected.

The community had changed as well.

Friday nights were full again, but steadier in the right ways. Parents stayed after the games. Players ate at the same houses year after year. Kids who never thought about football found a place in it.

Iron Valley had become dependable.

Jack turned toward the locker room as practice wrapped up, the echoes fading behind him.

The lessons stayed simple.

Build people before programs.
Teach process before results.
Stay when it's uncomfortable.
And never confuse winning with worth.

Jack started saying it when plans broke down.

The players turned it into a promise.

It went on shirts.
On signs.
All over town, when they mentioned Iron Valley.

FIND A WAY.

It wasn't motivation.

It was a reminder.

When things got hard, on the field or off, it was the same message.

No excuses.
No shortcuts.
Find a way.

Five years removed, Jack knew this for certain: the season that changed everything wasn't special because of what they won.

It mattered because of who they became.

And that was something no scoreboard could ever take away.

AUTHOR'S NOTE

This is a work of fiction.

Iron Valley isn't a real place.
West Ridge isn't a real rival.
The games, the scores, and the seasons are imagined.

But the people are real.

Every locker room I've ever been in has had a Marcus.
Every group has had a Tyler.
Every program has had a Neil: quiet, hurting, loyal, just trying to belong.

And every coach, whether they admit it or not, has been Jack at some point.

I didn't write this book to explain schemes or sell a system. There are plenty of books that do that better than I ever could. I wrote it because football already teaches us *how* to play, but far fewer people talk honestly about what it costs to stay.

Most programs don't fail because they don't know football.
They fail because panic replaces patience.
Because winning becomes louder than people.
Because nobody teaches what to do after losing.

The themes in this story: Trust, Discipline, Response, Redemption, and Composure, aren't slogans. They're survival tools. They're the things that keep a team together when the scoreboard doesn't cooperate, and the noise gets loud.

This story isn't about a perfect coach.
Jack gets it wrong more than once.
He hesitates. He doubts. He hurts people while trying to help them.

That's intentional.

Because leadership isn't about having the right answers, it's about staying long enough to learn better ones.

If you're a coach, I hope that this book reminds you that:

- Wins fade faster than impact
- Culture shows up in silence, not celebration
- And the most important work rarely happens on Friday night

If you're a parent or player, I hope it reminds you that:

- Progress isn't always visible
- People don't need saving; they need people who believe in them
- And showing up still counts

Iron Valley didn't change because of a playbook.

It changed because people chose to stay, to listen, and to value the process when results weren't guaranteed.

If this book causes you to slow down, to hold your composure one more rep, or to choose people over panic, then it did its job.

That's all it was ever meant to do.

DISCUSSION & REFLECTION QUESTIONS

For Coaches, Leaders, and Teams

This story wasn't written to provide answers, but to start conversations.

Throughout the season at Iron Valley, Coach Mercer introduced a single word each week to guide the team's focus.

The word wasn't meant to be a speech. It was meant to shape how the team practiced, played, and responded when things became difficult.

The words that follow come directly from the moments in this story.

Each theme represents a lesson the team had to learn along the way.

Coaches, players, and teams can use these pages in several ways:

Weekly Team Meeting

Choose one word and discuss the questions together as a team before practice.

Leadership Group

Captains or leadership councils can work through the themes and discuss how they apply to the team.

Individual Reflection

Players can read the chapter connected to each theme and reflect on the questions personally.

The goal is not to find perfect answers.

The goal is to think about the kind of team you want to become.

Great teams are rarely built on talent alone.

They are built on shared values that show up every day.

These were the words that helped shape Iron Valley.

Use these questions for reflection, staff discussion, or team leadership development.

The Words That Built Iron Valley:

Trust
Finish
Poise
Consistency
Answer
Redemption
Resilience
Accountability
Composure
Steady
Belief
Endure

Which word will define your team?

TRUST

Trust is believing in the preparation, the system, and the people beside you—even when the outcome is uncertain.

Early in the season, Iron Valley struggled because players tried to do everything themselves. As the team grew, they began trusting their roles, their teammates, and the preparation that had been built throughout the season.

Trust doesn't eliminate mistakes.
It allows teams to keep moving forward when mistakes happen.

Questions for Players

1. When is it hardest to trust your teammates during a game?

2. How does trust affect communication on the field?

3. What actions help build trust inside a team?

4. What actions destroy trust?

Questions for Coaches

1. How do coaches show trust in players?

2. Are there moments where players need more freedom to make decisions?

3. How can trust be built during practice, not just during games?

FINISH

Finish means completing the work even after the excitement fades.

Many teams start strong but fade when fatigue, frustration, or adversity arrives. Iron Valley learned that finishing well required discipline long after the scoreboard stopped being comfortable.

Finishing isn't about the final whistle.
It's about the habits that carry a team all the way there.

Questions for Players

1. What does finishing a play look like?

2. Why do some teams start fast but finish poorly?

3. How can teammates hold each other accountable to finishing drills?

Questions for Coaches

1. How do practice structures reinforce finishing?

2. Do players understand that finishing applies to academics and life too?

POISE

Poise is the ability to remain calm and disciplined when the moment becomes loud.

Football rarely unfolds exactly as planned. Momentum swings. Big plays happen. Injuries occur. Crowds get louder and emotions rise.

Iron Valley faced several moments during the season where panic could have taken over. Early in the year, mistakes sometimes stacked together because players tried to fix everything themselves. One bad play turned into another.

As the season went on, the team began to change. When adversity hit, they learned to pause between plays and reset.

Questions for Players

1. When during a game is it hardest to keep your poise?

2. What usually causes players to panic or rush decisions?

Questions for Coaches

1. Players often mirror the sideline. How can a coach's behavior influence a team's poise?

2. What practice situations can simulate pressure so players learn to stay calm?

3. When adversity hits, what message should players hear from their coaches first?

CONSISTENCY

Consistency means doing the right things over and over again.

Iron Valley's turnaround did not happen because of one big moment. It came from small habits repeated daily. Practice structure, preparation, and accountability slowly built the foundation for improvement.

Players began to understand that consistency builds confidence. When the same effort shows up every day, the results eventually follow.

Questions for Players

1. Why is consistency harder than motivation?
2. What habits help players stay consistent?
3. How does consistency build confidence on the field?

Questions for Coaches

1. How can coaches reinforce consistent habits?
2. What routines help players stay focused week after week?
3. How does consistency shape team culture?

ANSWER

Answer is how a team responds when adversity shows up.

Every game brings moments where things go wrong. A turnover. A penalty. A big play by the opponent.

Iron Valley learned that strong teams respond quickly instead of dwelling on mistakes. The next play becomes the focus. Players answer challenges by executing their job and helping the team move forward.

Questions for Players

1. What is the difference between reacting and responding?

2. How does a team's response affect momentum in a game?

3. What habits help players reset after mistakes?

Questions for Coaches

1. How can coaches help players move on from mistakes quickly?

2. What language reinforces a strong response during games?

3. How can leaders guide the team during difficult moments?

REDEMPTION

Redemption means growing beyond past mistakes.

Iron Valley carried the weight of losing seasons and difficult moments. Some players wondered if things would ever change.

As the season unfolded, redemption came through steady work and belief in each other. The past did not disappear, but it no longer defined the team.

Questions for Players

1. Why do past failures sometimes stay with teams?
2. How can players turn mistakes into motivation?
3. What role does redemption play in sports?

Questions for Coaches

1. How can coaches help players grow from failure?
2. What role does accountability play in redemption?
3. How do programs rebuild confidence after difficult seasons?

RESILIENCE

Resilience is the ability to keep moving forward after setbacks.

Iron Valley faced challenges throughout the season. Injuries, tough losses, and difficult games tested the team's resolve.

Resilient teams do not avoid adversity. They learn to push through it together and continue working toward improvement.

Questions for Players

1. What moments test a team's resilience the most?
2. How can teammates support each other through adversity?
3. Why is resilience important during a long season?

Questions for Coaches

1. How do coaches build resilience in players?
2. What experiences help teams develop mental toughness?
3. How do leaders respond when adversity hits?

ACCOUNTABILITY

Accountability means taking responsibility for actions and results.

As Iron Valley grew, players began holding themselves and each other to higher standards. Mistakes were no longer ignored or blamed on others.

Accountability created trust and helped the team move forward together.

Questions for Players

1. Why can accountability be difficult for teams?
2. How do leaders hold teammates accountable respectfully?
3. What happens when accountability disappears?

Questions for Coaches

1. How can coaches model accountability?
2. What systems reinforce team standards?
3. How do you correct mistakes while maintaining confidence?

COMPOSURE

Composure is emotional control during critical moments.

Football games are full of intense situations. Big plays, penalties, and crowd reactions can quickly raise emotions.

Iron Valley learned that maintaining composure helped players stay focused on the next play instead of getting caught up in the moment.

Questions for Players

1. What situations challenge composure during games?
2. How can teammates help restore composure?
3. Why is emotional control important in competition?

Questions for Coaches

1. How can coaches help players regain composure?
2. What practice situations prepare players for emotional moments?
3. How does composure influence leadership?

STEADY

Steady means maintaining focus regardless of circumstances.

Throughout the season, Iron Valley discovered that progress came from staying steady through both wins and losses. Emotional swings often hurt teams more than the scoreboard.

Steady leadership helped the team remain focused on improvement instead of reacting to outside pressure.

Questions for Players

1. What does steady leadership look like?
2. How do emotional swings affect teams?
3. How can players stay steady during difficult games?

Questions for Coaches

1. How can coaches create stability during tough seasons?
2. What habits help teams stay steady?
3. How do leaders influence the emotional tone of a team?

BELIEF

Belief is the foundation of a successful team.

Iron Valley's season began to change when players started believing improvement was possible. Belief did not come from words alone. It grew through preparation, trust, and shared effort.

As belief grew, so did confidence.

Questions for Players

1. When does belief begin to grow within a team?
2. How does belief influence effort and confidence?
3. What actions strengthen belief among teammates?

Questions for Coaches

1. How can coaches build belief during difficult seasons?
2. What moments strengthen belief in a program?
3. How does belief affect performance?

ENDURE

Endure means continuing forward when the outcome is uncertain.

Playoff football tested Iron Valley physically and emotionally. Injuries, pressure, and tough opponents pushed the team to its limits.

Endurance required players to keep showing up, competing, and supporting each other even when the path became difficult.

Questions for Players

1. What does endurance look like during a long season?
2. Why do some teams fade late in the year?
3. How can teammates support each other when things get difficult?

Questions for Coaches

1. How can practices prepare players to endure pressure?
2. What habits help teams stay strong late in the season?
3. How does endurance translate beyond sports?

I. For Coaches & Leaders

1. The scoreboard doesn't care—but how often do your decisions still revolve around it?

2. Where is your program built on habit instead of emotion?

3. Jack learns that hard work alone wasn't enough. Where might you be busy but misaligned?

4. Who are the quiet players in your program—and do they feel seen?

5. What standards in your program only work when you are present?

6. When has patience been mistaken for softness—or toughness mistaken for leadership?

7. What is the cost of real culture change in your environment?

8. After losses, do you fix problems—or reflect on foundations?

9. Which leadership habits come from your past rather than your principles?

10. If winning disappeared tomorrow, what would still remain?

II. For Staffs or Book Studies

1. Which chapter challenged your comfort the most—and why?
2. Where did Jack make a decision that would be unpopular in your setting?
3. How does this story redefine accountability?
4. What moments showed belief forming before results?
5. How did silence communicate more than speeches?
6. Which character modeled leadership without authority?
7. What role did consistency play when pressure increased?
8. How did trust change staff dynamics?
9. What would one shared weekly theme change in your program?
10. How do you protect culture when outside voices grow louder?

III. For Players & Team Leaders

1. What does "doing your job" mean when no one is watching?
2. When have you stayed physically present but checked out mentally?

3. Who do you trust on your team—and why?

4. What does leadership look like when you're not the star?

5. How do you respond when life affects your performance?

6. Who has helped carry your weight when it was heavy?

7. What does "staying" mean to you?

8. How do your actions affect teammates who don't speak up?

9. What kind of teammate are you after mistakes?

10. What will your teammates remember about how you showed up?

Closing Reflection

Your Iron Valley

What does your team stand for?
What will you refuse to quit on?
Who needs you to stay, especially when it's hard?

Books That Informed This Story

While *Iron Valley* is a work of fiction, its themes, coaching philosophy, and leadership moments are drawn directly from ideas developed across the following books.

Coaching Football Like a Basketball Coach

Core influence

This book shaped the story's emphasis on:

- Teaching in layers
- Adjusting without panic
- Using structure to create freedom
- Coaches as teachers, not just play-callers

Jack's approach to practice design, staff meetings, and in-game adjustments reflects this philosophy throughout the novel.

Find a Way

Emotional and leadership backbone

This book directly informed:

- The idea of staying when it's hard
- Belief before results
- Leaders who don't quit on people

Jack's internal doubts, persistence through losing, and refusal to abandon players after failure are rooted in this mindset.

Training for More Than the Game

"Beyond the Game" themes

This book shaped:

- Weekly team themes
- The focus on character, response, and growth
- Coaches impacting lives outside the lines

Much of the Marcus, Neil, and family-centered storytelling flows from this foundation.

0–10 to 10-0 – Lessons Learned in Coaching

Failure as a coach

This book informed:

- The reality of losing seasons
- How programs often grow before they win
- The danger of chasing results too fast

Jack's first season, doubt, and long view of growth are directly tied to these lessons.

Final Note

This story was not written to teach *what to run.*

It was written to remind coaches and players:

- Why they coach and play
- Who they coach or play for
- And what matters when winning isn't guaranteed

Every book above provided a piece of that truth.

This novel simply told it in story form.

ABOUT THE AUTHOR

Kenny Simpson is a veteran high school football coach with 22 seasons of experience, including 17 as a head coach. He currently serves as the head football coach at Southside Charter High School in Batesville, Arkansas, in his second tenure at the program. Taking over a team that had won just eight games in five seasons and endured a 20-plus game losing streak, Coach Simpson helped transform Southside into a consistent contender, leading to multiple conference championships and seven playoff appearances in recent years. His work earned him 4A-2 Conference Coach of the Year honors in 2017 and 2024, finalist recognition for Hooten's Coach of the Year in those same seasons, and nominations to coach in the Arkansas High School All-Star Game (2023) and the FCA Texas-Arkansas All-Star Showdown (2021).

Previously, Coach Simpson served as head coach at Searcy High School, a 6A program in Arkansas, and at Alabama Christian Academy in Montgomery, Alabama, where he guided a 4–18 program to its first home playoff game in more than two decades. He was named Montgomery Advertiser All-Metro Coach of the Year and 4A Region 2 Coach of the Year in 2010. His coaching career began at Madison Academy in Huntsville, Alabama, where he started as a junior high basketball and football coach before moving into varsity football. He is a graduate of Harding University.

He is the author of more than 40 books and a 15-time bestselling author, first reaching Amazon bestseller status with *Find a Way: What I Wish I'd Known When I Became a Head Football Coach*. His writing spans leadership, program building, fundraising, and offensive and defensive systems, all rooted in real-world experience. He is also the creator of the Gun-T RPO Offensive System, a modern adaptation of Wing-T principles blended with spread concepts, now used by programs across the United States and internationally.

Through FBCoachSimpson.com, GunTSystem.com, OffensiveCoordinatorAcademy.com, DefensiveCoordinatorAcademy.com, and TheHeadCoachAcademy.com, Coach Simpson provides playbooks, manuals, academies, memberships, digital courses, and mentoring resources designed to help coaches build systems that fit their players and communities. He has also helped raise more than $1.5 million for facility improvements at Southside Charter, including FieldTurf installation, fieldhouse expansions, bleachers, a press box, and a video board.

Coach Simpson believes coaching is a calling rooted in service, consistency, and responsibility beyond the scoreboard. Much of his work—whether in *Iron Valley*, the Gun-T series, or his leadership titles—focuses on the grind of rebuilding, the power of belief and process, and the quiet impact that comes from staying invested in people when things get hard.

He lives in Arkansas with his wife, Jamey, a two-time author, and their three children, Avery, Braden, and Bennett, continuing to coach, write, and equip the next generation of football leaders.

BOOKS FROM THIS AUTHOR

Find A Way: What I Wish I'd Known When I Became A Head Football Coach

Coaching Football Like A Basketball Coach

Training Athletes Beyond The Game

Athletic Fundraising

Team Themes – Volumes 1, 2, 3, 4, and 5

One Play Many Ways: Teaching Conceptual Football

10 Hard Lessons Learned In Coaching

The Playcaller's Guide

0-10 To 10-0

Complete Guide To Buck Sweep From The Shotgun

GUN T SYSTEM BOOKS

Gun T Playbook
Gun T 2.0
Gun T Organizational Manual
Gun T Offensive Line Manual
Gun T Youth Manual
Gun T 3.0
Gun T 4.0
Gun T 5.0
Gun T 6.0
Gun T 7.0
Gun T Offensive Line Drill Book
Gun T Offensive Line Manual
Gun T Wide Receiver Manual
Gun T Youth Drill Book
Gun T QB Manual

Defensive Books

34 Fit and Swarm Overview
34 Fit and Swarm Organizational Manual
34 Fit and Swarm Defensive Line Manual
34 Fit and Swarm Youth Organizational Manual

Coaching Academy Books

Head Coach, Offensive Coordinator, Defensive Coordinator Workbooks and Planners

Defensive Line Coach – Workbook
Offensive Line Coach – Workbook
Quarterback Coach - Workbook

www.ingramcontent.com/pod-product-compliance
Lightning Source LLC
LaVergne TN
LVHW020649110826
845149LV00012B/1955

9798995341109